CABIN
FEVER

USA TODAY Bestselling Author

KAREN ROSE SMITH

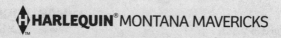

H HARLEQUIN® MONTANA MAVERICKS

Special thanks and acknowledgment are given to Karen Rose Smith for her contribution to the MONTANA MAVERICKS: GOLD RUSH GROOMS miniseries.

ISBN-13: 978-0-373-41811-4

Cabin Fever

Copyright © 2005 by Harlequin Books S.A.

Recycling programs for this product may not exist in your area.

Printed in U.S.A.

Award-winning author **Karen Rose Smith** has sold over eighty books since 1991. Since then her romance novels have made both the *USA TODAY* bestseller list and the Amazon Contemporary Romance bestseller list. Believing in the power of love, she envisions herself writing relationship novels for a long time to come! Readers can email Karen through her website at karenrosesmith.com or follow her on Twitter, @karenrosesmith, and on Facebook, Karen Rose Smith Author.

To my continuity partners,
Christine Rimmer, Allison Leigh, Pam Toth,
Judy Duarte and Cheryl St.John,
who made working on this project a pleasure.

With thanks to Jessica Miller for her valuable help
in describing Montana weather and scenery.
Her love of the state easily inspired me.

Chapter One

"I am *not* the father," Brad Vaughn stated in no uncertain terms.

The Chicago private investigation firm of Vaughn Associates was *not* where Brad wanted to have this discussion. However, with his dad standing in his office, newspaper in hand, Brad had no choice.

Phillip Vaughn, head of the firm, a man who was always right, a father who was grooming his son for his position, shook the newspaper at Brad. "Are you sure? Suzette Brouchard says—"

"I don't care what Suzette Brouchard says.

We had a brief relationship, but I never slept with her without protection. From the information I have so far, her baby was born forty-two weeks after our last night together. She'd moved on to someone else, and *that* man is the father of her baby."

Suzette was a beautiful, sexy model, but neither of them had expected more than a few nights of good sex. She'd faded into the background after they'd stopped seeing each other, and that had been almost three years ago.

"Why would she do this?" Phillip Vaughn asked, still in an accusing tone.

"Money. She thinks if she makes enough noise, I'll settle and give her a bundle."

Brad *had* a bundle. Not from the fortune his father had acquired but from his own sweat. He'd earned an MBA and opted out of his father's plans for him for a few years to work on Wall Street. He'd done well and invested most of it, not in the dot-com of the moment but in solid, stable companies he'd researched. At the height of the boom, he'd sold most of it, bought real estate, sold that, reinvested in conservative investments for the future and constantly turned over the rest for profit. At thirty-five, he had more money than he'd ever need.

Money certainly hadn't been the reason he'd joined his father in his firm. Taking over Vaughn Associates someday hadn't been one of his aspirations. However, when his mother had phoned him and gently suggested his dad wouldn't be around forever, Brad had wondered if he and his father could set aside the adversarial relationship they'd always had and forge real bonds they could build on. But Brad had been vice president of his dad's firm for two years now, and the bonds were as thready as they'd always been. He didn't know any more now what made Phillip Vaughn tick than he had when he was twelve and his parents had divorced.

"I've already contacted Suzette's lawyer and informed him I'll be giving a sample for a DNA test today. This will be settled within a month," Brad said decisively.

"The reputation of this firm could suffer a hell of a lot in a month if articles like this keep appearing."

"That's what Suzette and her lawyer are counting on."

"A settlement could shut it all down *today,*" Phillip insisted.

But Brad wasn't about to settle, not when his reputation was at stake. "No. I want to clear my name. I won't be thought of as an irresponsible playboy who doesn't care if he gets a woman pregnant."

"That's not what you are?" his father asked with a bit of an amused smile.

His dad often frustrated him. Now his question rankled in a deep place that unsettled Brad. "I have *never* been irresponsible."

Silence reverberated in the office until his father broke it. "Maybe you should think about settling down," he suggested, throwing the newspaper onto Brad's mahogany desk.

"You know how I feel about that." Brad couldn't keep the acerbic edge from his voice.

When his father had kicked his mother out of their home after her affair, Brad had lived with her during the week and with his father on weekends. He wouldn't take the chance of doing that to any kid. Besides that, he simply didn't trust women. That might have started with his mother's infidelity, but in college he'd given the fairer sex a chance. That had been a mistake. His father had bought off the girl that he didn't deem appropriate for Brad, and Brad's eyes had been opened to exactly how little love mattered compared to the allure of money.

"With your paternity up in the air, what are you going to do about Thunder Canyon?" his father asked.

"Thunder Canyon can't wait," Brad answered, considering the client's case he was personally overseeing.

Thunder Canyon, Montana, was a small town near Bozeman. Since Vaughn Associates was acclaimed for its security work and all-around private investigation skill, the company's reputation was known across the country. Caleb Douglas, one of the most renowned citizens of Thunder Canyon, had hired Vaughn Associates to uncover the true ownership of a gold mine there.

"I got the history from Caleb Douglas yesterday," Brad went on. "Since the late eighteen hundreds, the Douglas family has claimed the property in Thunder Canyon that includes the Queen of Hearts gold mine. Now they can't find the deed. Caleb has always assumed he knew the truth and the land was his. I'm hoping I can wrap up the investigation in a few days."

A small voice on his shoulder, however, reminded him a missing deed could mean trouble.

"I'll need to find the deed or some proof of ownership. I'm going to ask Emily to go along."

"Your secretary? Is she necessary?"

"Caleb said he wanted this done quickly no matter how much it cost. If Emily's along, I can count on her to write up the daily reports and do preliminary interviews."

With a frown, his father checked his watch. "I have an appointment across town. I'd better get going." He cast a disdainful glance at the newspaper once more. "Maybe if you're out of town for a few days, the hubbub over that...situation...will settle down. I don't want to have to field calls about your personal life while you're away."

As if his father really knew anything about his personal life. "If you receive any calls, give the caller my cell number," Brad said curtly.

Phillip gave him a long look. "I'll do just that." Then he left Brad's office.

Crossing to the doorway, Brad's gaze didn't follow his father as he left the office suite. Rather, his eyes rested on Emily Stan-

ton. His secretary sat at her computer, headset on, transcribing yesterday's reports.

Brad would never depend on a woman in
his personal life. He knew the foolishness,
the futility in that. But in his professional
life, Emily was as dependable as a woman
got. She was organized, punctual, thorough
and sometimes uncannily able to read his
mind. With her straight, dark brown hair—
shoulder length and blunt—her bangs; her
sedate, always-polite attitude, she didn't turn
heads and she didn't flirt. She was just available when he needed her, straightforward in
her manner and an asset he didn't want to
contemplate doing without. She'd been with
the Vaughn secretarial pool for two years.
Then, six months ago, when his secretary
had taken maternity leave, Emily had applied for the promotion. He knew from her
personnel records she was twenty-seven, but
he didn't know much else. They'd never had
a personal discussion.

Engrossed in her work, Emily wasn't even
aware of him stepping out of his office. Since
she was wearing her headset, he clasped her
shoulder, hoping not to startle her. "Emily?"

She gasped and came up out of her chair
so fast her headset flew from her ears and

landed on the computer keyboard. They were standing toe to toe and almost nose to nose, except her nose came to the knot of his tie. He suddenly realized how petite and fragile she seemed as he inhaled a flowery scent—lilacs, maybe? Yes, Emily Stanton smelled like lilacs. Had he ever been this close to her before?

Trying to back up, she bumped into the desk. "Mr. Vaughn! Did you call me? I didn't hear you come out of your office."

"No, I didn't call you." He motioned to the headset. "I didn't think you'd hear me."

She was wearing a two-piece black suit today, with a boxy jacket and a straight skirt. For the first time since he'd hired her, he noticed her eyes were the color of emeralds.

For a moment, neither of them spoke, just gazed at each other.

Then, feeling a bit unsettled and not knowing exactly why, Brad asked, "Can you come into my office? There's something I need to discuss with you."

Emily's cheeks were flushed and she didn't appear to be her calm, cool self as she reached for the legal pad on her desk and a pen in the holder. "Sure. I'll be right in."

Brad didn't wait but returned to his office

and lowered himself into the tall, burgundy leather chair behind his desk.

Hurrying in after him, Emily took a seat in one of the two chairs facing him. She was composed again, her legal pad and pen ready to take notes or directions. Emily loved lists, he knew. She stuck them on her computer, on her keyboard, on her desk. He supposed that's how she stayed organized.

"I have a special assignment for you. Something out of the ordinary."

"A special assignment?" she repeated, looking perplexed.

"Remember those notes you typed on Caleb Douglas?"

"The man who thinks he owns a gold mine in Montana?"

"He's the one. By the way, thanks for staying late last night and deciphering my scribblings from the phone call with him."

There were still spots of color on her cheeks. "No problem. I knew you wanted to start working on his case today."

"There's some urgency in finding out whether he truly owns this mine or not. Supposedly the gold mine was abandoned in the late eighteen hundreds. But a couple of months ago, when a young boy fell down an erosion hole into a mine canal, gold nuggets were found. Caleb Douglas, of course, wants to mine any gold if it's there. The problem is, he and his family can't find the deed."

"And you're supposed to find it?"

"I'm supposed to find out who truly owns the Queen of Hearts mine. I doubt if I'll find the deed itself, but hopefully I can find some type of record that will prove Caleb Douglas is the rightful heir or the owner."

"What do you want *me* to do?"

As Brad's attention focused on Emily again and the expectant look on her face, he realized how cute she actually was. Was he looking at her differently because he'd be traveling with her? Because he was thinking about time they'd be spending together outside of the office? Because he was thinking about how she'd look in blue jeans?

Reminding himself that Emily wasn't the type of woman he dated for a multitude of reasons, he said evenly, "I'd like you to fly to Montana with me tomorrow. As I said, I need to tie up this case quickly. If you're along, the work might go faster. We might have to page through a lot of old records, and I may need to follow leads while you make calls."

Her gaze dropped to his desk and the newspaper lying there. Then she asked, "It would just be you and me? Alone?"

Brad had the reputation for being one of the most eligible bachelors in Chicago. He had been dubbed that when a reporter had written an article about him after he'd returned to his hometown. At the time it hadn't bothered him, but now he didn't like that reputation any more than he liked the column that had appeared about him and Suzette in this morning's paper.

Picking up the newspaper, he folded it in half and tossed it into the trash can beside his desk. "The allegations are false."

To her credit, Emily didn't play dumb. "It's none of my business," she said softly.

"You're my secretary. It's your business because I don't want unfounded gossip to keep you from taking this trip."

"I'm surprised you're going away now," she admitted honestly.

"I'm not going to let an unsubstantiated accusation interfere with my work or with my life."

"I don't know, Mr. Vaughn…."

"It's only for a few days, Emily. There will be plenty of other people around. We'll be busy with interviews and public records."

"Where would we stay?"

"There's an inn and a motel. From what I understand, it's pretty much a little, one-horse town, but it's readying itself for a new ski resort."

Seeing indecision still on her face, he offered the one incentive he knew she'd understand and probably not resist. "If you take this trip to Thunder Canyon with me, I'll toss in a bonus." He named a sum that made her eyes widen.

"You're willing to pay that much for my help?"

"I'm willing to pay that for *good* help. I need someone dependable, and you're dependable. So what do you say?"

After a few moments of hesitation, she asked, "When should I be ready to leave?"

"Sorry, Mr. Vaughn, I simply have no rooms to rent you," said the motel manager with a Texas drawl that seemed out of place in Montana.

Emily couldn't believe what she and Brad were hearing. He had told her yesterday there was no need to make advance reservations since the tourist season wasn't yet in full swing. They'd just arrived at dinnertime, and they were worn out from their flight—from Chicago to Denver, then Denver to Bozeman. The foreman of Caleb Douglas's ranch had picked them up at the airport and driven them to Thunder Canyon. When he'd asked where they wanted to go, Brad had directed him to the Big Sky Motel at the edge of town.

Standing to one side, the foreman of the Lazy D—a man in his fifties with a stubble of gray beard and a huge black Stetson— tipped his hat up on his forehead. "It's because of the gold rush. We got more people coming in than this town knows what to do with."

"Mr. Vaughn, maybe we should try to call Caleb Douglas," Emily suggested.

"It's Brad, Emily. I told you that on the plane. And Caleb Douglas is going to be meeting us here anytime now." Turning back to the hotel clerk, he demanded, "Let me talk to the manager."

Emily could tell Brad was getting impatient. He was the type of man who was used to clearing his way no matter what the obstacles in his path.

The man behind the desk looked a bit frazzled, too. Emily thought he looked a little like Al Pacino. He wore a name tag that said Jess Anderson.

Now the motel manager tugged on his bolo tie and blew out a breath. "I'm the manager *and* the owner. I don't have any rooms to give you."

Taking his wallet from his jeans, Brad removed a bill. Emily's breath caught when she saw that it was a hundred dollars. Her employer laid it on the counter. "Are you sure?"

Mr. Anderson seemed to draw himself up a little straighter, not that he was anywhere near Brad Vaughn's six-foot-three height. Emily sensed a tirade coming on.

With her best friendly smile and her calmest voice, she stepped up a little closer to Brad and then was sorry she did. Even at the end of the day, she could smell a trace scent of cologne. His short, black, curly hair was a bit mussed, and beard stubble darkened his jaw. She should know better than to get too close to him. She avoided men like Brad when they crossed her path, and she wasn't about to be stranded in a strange town with him with no place to sleep for the night.

Emily fingered the strap of the camera bag that was hanging around her neck. "Mr. Anderson, I can see you're busy, but we've come a long way. Could you recommend some-place else we could try? A bed-and-break-fast maybe?"

"No bed-and-breakfasts around here. There's a dude ranch on the edge of town. I sent some folks over there yesterday, but now they're full up, too. You should have called first."

"I never expected this place to be over-flowing with tourists," Brad told the motel owner.

Mr. Anderson shook his head. "I've never seen anything like it. All this because a cou-ple of people found a few little nuggets of gold." He glanced at Emily again. "Let me make a few calls, miss." Pushing Brad's hundred-dollar bill back at him, he said haughtily, "No need for that."

Putting the bill back where it belonged, Brad looked puzzled, as if he didn't under-stand what the hotel owner had just done.

When Emily had applied for the job with Brad Vaughn, she'd put her attraction to him aside, keeping her eye on the promo-tion. There had been a buzz about his return to Chicago. Everyone knew Phillip Vaughn was grooming him to take over someday, but Brad wasn't the kind of man to be groomed.

She'd passed him in the halls, glimpsed him picking up work at the secretarial pool. Her heart had thudded riotously every time she had. He was the kind of man women noticed.

But she'd had her fill of that kind of man. As the old adage went, *Once burned, twice shy.* She'd emerged from her first and only serious relationship with more than a broken heart. She'd been devastated. Not because she'd found herself pregnant and the man had walked away but because a few weeks later she'd had a miscarriage. She didn't want handsome, wealthy, irresponsible men anywhere near her radar screen. She had a sister to finish putting through college and she had her own goals now. Nothing was going to interfere with them.

Not even her elemental reaction to her sexy boss.

"What seems to be the problem?" a booming voice asked over Emily's shoulder.

She turned and found a man in his sixties with silver hair, pale green eyes and a ruddy face that looked as if he spent a lot of time outdoors. His white Stetson sat high on his forehead and his turquoise-and-silver belt buckle caught the glimmer of the overhead lights as he unbuttoned his suede jacket.

Emily wished she'd brought along *her* suede jacket. She'd never realized May in Montana would not be the same as May in Chicago. It still felt like winter here.

The foreman pointed to Brad. "This here's your private investigator."

Caleb Douglas extended his hand to Brad. "It's good to meet you, son."

"It's good to meet you, too, Mr. Douglas." Then, to Emily's surprise, Brad nodded to her. "This is Emily Stanton, my assistant."

Caleb reached for her hand and pumped it, too. "How do you do, Miss Stanton."

"I'm fine, thank you. Anxious to get to work. But we do have a problem. There aren't any rooms. Mr. Anderson is making a few calls—"

Jess Anderson returned to the front desk to face Brad once more. "I'm sorry, Mr. Vaughn, there's just nothing in this town to rent. You might have to drive back to Bozeman."

"No sense in that," Caleb decided. "Under any other circumstances, I'd invite you to stay with me at the ranch, but my wife's family is visiting from back east. They haven't visited for ten years and all of a sudden they came roaring in like a herd of cattle gone crazy. All because of the gold rush. Anyway, like I said, you can't stay at the ranch right now, but I bought a cabin last month to get away from all this hullabaloo. It's about forty minutes out of town, up in the mountains. I've only been there a few times and I haven't had time to get it renovated yet. But the essentials are there. My wife's family should be leaving in a few days, and then you'll be welcome to stay with me. In the meantime, maybe Mr. Anderson will have a vacancy. What do you think?"

To her dismay, Emily felt as if she were riding a train to an unwanted destination. It was going too fast for her to jump off. One minute she'd been sitting at her desk, typing up Brad's notes, and the next she was facing a night in a cozy cabin with Brad. Alone.

No way.

"I don't know if that would be a good idea," she began, trying to be calm, reasonable and professional.

To Caleb, Brad said, "Will you excuse us for a minute?" Clasping Emily's elbow, he pulled her aside.

After Brad had tugged her a good five feet away, he said in a low voice, "This offer's the best one we've got."

"I can't spend the night *alone* in a cabin

with you. What would my family say? What would your father say?"

"You're twenty-seven, Emily. Your family cares if you spend the night alone in a cabin with a man?"

"I have an older brother who's protective. I have two younger sisters who I have to set an example for."

Brad was looking at her as if she'd landed in Thunder Canyon from another planet.

"They care about me, Mr.—" she felt Brad's warning look "—Brad."

"Do you think they'd rather have you spend the night in a car or maybe Caleb Douglas's barn?"

When Emily worked for Brad, she concentrated hard on her work and didn't let him distract her. Today she hadn't had work to concentrate on. Whenever he looked at her, her breath caught. The feel of his hand on her arm was making her whole body tingle. His presence sent her into a tizzy and that's why she couldn't think straight. She could see now they really didn't have any other options.

The fact that he couldn't convince her easily had made Brad's jaw set. If he was angry with her, he was restraining it well as the sparks in his eyes made butterflies dance in her stomach.

Finally he released her arm. "If you want to return to Chicago, I'll find someone to take you to Bozeman. But I doubt if there are any flights out tonight."

She was sure he was right about that and, darn it, she wanted that bonus. She needed it to help with the last of her sister's expenses. After Lizbeth graduated, Emily could save toward going to college herself. "I don't want to go back to Chicago. I came here to do a job with you and I'm going to do it. Let's tell Mr. Douglas we'll stay at his cabin."

"Are you sure?" Brad's deep voice held a measure of concern.

Before she lost her nerve, she responded, "Yes, I'm sure."

When Caleb's foreman dropped Brad and Emily off at the rental-and-used-car lot, Brad still had high expectations this trip would be quick and successful. Now he hoped so even more than before. Cooped up in planes beside Emily for most of the day, he'd been much too affected by her natural femininity. There was nothing coy about her, nothing flirtatious, nothing pretentious. But ever since yesterday, he couldn't keep the adrenaline from rushing through him whenever he inadvertently touched her. He couldn't keep the light scent of her perfume from teasing his libido.

However, self-restraint had never been a problem. So they were going to spend the night in the cabin together. It was one night, and he'd pretend she was a backpacking buddy.

Emily had insisted on staying outside with the luggage and the laptop computer he'd brought along mainly for her use. Inside a small building on the car lot, Brad's expectations diminished as he spoke to the woman behind the desk. She'd just told him she had no SUVs to rent.

"If you don't have an SUV, what about a pickup?"

The frizzy-haired redhead frowned. "Mister, you've got to understand what's happening here. We've got more sightseers than you can count coming into Thunder Canyon. Up until a few months ago, we didn't have much call for rentals. Now we can't keep an SUV or a truck on the lot to rent or sell. I can take your name and number, and if one comes in I can call you. But for now, that blue sedan out there is as good as it gets. It was turned in yesterday and the mechanic went over it before he left today, so it's in good shape."

Peering out the window, Brad spotted the light blue midsize car. He produced his credit card, knowing he had no choice. "I'll take it."

When he emerged from the office ten minutes later, keys in hand, he noticed the big, blue Montana sky had changed. Gray clouds had covered the sun although dusk was still an hour away. He was starved and he supposed Emily was, too. She was standing by their luggage, her arms wrapped around herself.

She hadn't dressed for Montana weather. For their flight she'd worn tan casual slacks and a cream oxford shirt. But the blouse had short sleeves, and the sweater she'd thrown over her arms for most of the trip didn't look that heavy. He'd spent a summer in Montana over a decade ago, but he'd forgotten the weather here was as changeable as a woman's moods. He'd forgotten how even in summer the mornings could have a nip and the nighttime temperature could drop into the fifties.

He dangled the keys in front of her and lifted her suitcase, as well as his. "I have directions to a grocery store. We can pick up food and supplies and head out. Do you have the directions Caleb gave us?"

An open Jeep with four men sitting inside sped much too quickly down the street. The vehicle backfired as it turned a corner.

Hoisting her purse onto her shoulder, Emily took a slip of paper from her pocket as she tried to keep up with his long stride. "Right here. I went over them again. We're going to have to watch the odometer carefully. He said there weren't any road signs after the first turnoff. How rustic do you think this cabin is?"

"He said there's one bedroom and the place is furnished. There's water and electricity, but if the power goes out, we have to use the pump out back for water."

Emily was horrified. "If the electricity goes out?"

He stopped. "It's in the mountains, Emily. I guess anything can happen. Haven't you ever gone camping?"

Shaking her head, her expression told him that going on a camping trip was as foreign to her as signing up for a trip to Mars.

"Caleb assured me there's a fireplace. We'll be fine. We just have to remember to pick up some Sterno."

"Sterno?"

"So we can cook if the power goes out." He started walking again, came to the car and gave it a look-over. "It's not what I wanted but it should get us where we want to go."

"I hope so," she murmured, looking worried.

Before he thought better of it, he set the suitcases on the ground near the trunk and took a step closer to her. "We can handle anything for one night, right?"

A breeze whipped her hair across her face and a strand caught on her lip. Without forethought, he reached out and smoothed it away. Her skin was so soft under his thumb, her lips such a pretty natural pink, her eyes a shade of green that captivated him.

The hum between them that had seemed to come from nowhere kept him immobilized for a few seconds until finally she repeated bravely, "I can handle anything for one night."

But Brad was beginning to wonder whether *he* could.

A cabin in the mountains of Montana with a secretary he was suddenly finding very difficult to ignore. Bringing Emily Stanton along on this trip had been a monumental mistake. Now he just had to be damned sure he didn't make another one.

Chapter Two

Buying supplies took longer than it should have, Brad thought, as he drove away from the Old Town section of Thunder Canyon, with its frontierlike connected storefronts and boardwalk promenade. It seemed his taste and Emily's were decidedly different. She'd looked for food with few preservatives and spent more time in the produce section than he'd spent buying Sterno burners, matches, candles and a flashlight. While he'd snatched up a package of chocolate cookies, she'd weighed one apple against another. Now she was silent as the gray clouds faded into a dark sky and the wind picked up even more.

The interior of the car seemed much too confining with the heater blowing and Emily's perfume floating around him on the air currents. She was studying the map with a penlight attached to her key ring.

They were only a mile out of town when snow began to fall. It swirled lightly at first, then began hitting the windshield more densely.

"How can it be snowing?" Emily asked in amazement. "It's May."

"This is Montana."

"That explains it?"

"It's the altitude and the mountains and weather fronts. There *is* life outside of Chicago."

He hadn't meant to snap at her, but her dismay was evident, and he asked, "You're sorry you came, aren't you?"

"Aren't *you?*"

As tall firs collecting the swirling snow sped by, he realized he'd needed this break from routine. "Actually, I'm not. I get tired of sitting at the computer doing searches. I'm beginning to hate the politics of finessing important clients. And I'm thoroughly fed up with investigating one company stealing another's secrets."

In the darkness he could sense her gaze on him as she asked, "Isn't that what you want to be doing? Isn't that why you came back to Chicago and joined your father's firm?"

Emily had never asked him personal questions before. They'd never had a personal conversation, and he wasn't sure this was the right one to begin with. "I came back for lots of reasons," he answered, explaining nothing.

A few heartbeats passed as snow swept around the car in a squall, covering the road and everything else they couldn't see through the storm.

"Don't you like working with your father?"

Persistence with her work was one thing. Persistence in digging personal info out of him was another. "I came back to work with my father."

"That's not what I asked you. Sometimes you seem so removed from it all."

Day after day he'd thought Emily had done her work, not noticing much else. Apparently he'd been wrong. "It's not always easy working with family. When I'm in my office, I'm there to get a job done."

"You're good at what you do. You always

find the answer, solve the problem, connect the right people together."

"But…?" he drawled, knowing there was one.

"But you do it so…impersonally."

"The same way you do your work?" he inquired calmly.

Her hand brushed his question aside as she shifted in her seat to look at him. "That's different. I type. I file. I transcribe. I don't work with people. *You* do."

Thinking about it, he realized why he stayed impersonal. "It's no fun discovering that a wife is cheating on her husband. Why would I want to get involved?"

"You don't normally take divorce cases. At least not unless your client is rich and famous."

Brad remembered the talk-show host who had come to him last year asking for complete anonymity. Brad had met with the man where he could remain incognito, and Emily had set up those clandestine appointments.

Through the illumination of the car's headlights, Brad could hardly see ten feet in front of him. He slowed the vehicle to a crawl and glanced at the odometer. "I don't want to miss the first turn."

"I don't know how you can even see," Emily said in a subdued voice, dropping the subject they'd been discussing.

Brad wasn't sure he *could* see, but somehow through the snow he spotted the high and square rock formation that Caleb had described as distinctive right before the first turn. However, as he attempted to turn left, the car skidded, then spun in a circle.

In the dark, suspended moment, he heard Emily's gasp.

"We're all right," he assured her as he managed to control the car and head in the right direction again. Reaching out, he laid his hand on her arm.

When there wasn't another peep out of her, he stole a glance at her. "Are you okay?"

"No, I'm *not* okay," she blurted out. "I'm scared. What if we get stranded out here?"

"The snow's letting up. We're not going to get stranded. Why don't you try to find something on the radio."

"Do you think that's going to distract me?"

"It might distract us both."

In spite of his attempt to keep his attention focused on road conditions, to his annoyance *she* was distracting him...more than the storm or the snow or the wind or the strange road at night. Her reactions were so damned honest. He wasn't used to honesty from a woman.

Emily fiddled with the channel-selection knob on the radio, but all she could produce was static.

"I could hum," he suggested, trying to lighten the atmosphere. But Emily's mind was obviously still on their drive and their destination.

"What did you think of Caleb Douglas?" she asked, her voice not quite steady. He had to give her a gold star for trying to overcome her apprehension.

"I think he's a man with a lot on his plate. He has an office in town to run his new ski-resort project and he owns the biggest ranch in the area. But he still had to buy a cabin to find peace and quiet. That tells me his life is speeding by pretty fast and he's trying to put on the brakes."

Shifting in her seat again, she let go of her clench on the door handle. "Maybe. Or maybe he just needs a quiet place where he can get in touch with who he is, not who everyone *thinks* he is."

Emily's perceptive comment made Brad glance at her once more. Although he really couldn't see her by the luminescent glow of the dials, he was very much aware that she was there and that she had more substance than he ever expected. Still, he remembered the way she'd jumped at the offer of a bonus. He remembered the night his fiancée had let money take precedence over a life together with him. He remembered his lawyer telling him before he left Chicago, "Suzette Brouchard wants a settlement."

As Brad drove deeper and higher into the mountains, snow fell lightly most of the time. Now and then it became heavier and Brad could feel Emily's tension. That was an odd thing. He didn't consider himself particularly intuitive when it came to women because he didn't usually plug in that well.

By the time they reached the last turnoff on the directions, Brad felt relieved. "We're almost there."

Emily muttered, "Thank goodness," and he smiled. They'd laugh about this when they got back to Chicago.

In the next few moments, the smile slipped from Brad's lips. As he spotted the creek he'd have to cross before they drove the last half mile or so to the cabin, he realized the situation they'd be in if he did. In May, runoff from the mountains could cause flooding. As the road curved onto the bridge, he could see sloshing water had reached its snow-covered surface. The problem was, he couldn't turn back. With the snow accumulating steadily every mile they'd traveled, the car would never manage a trip back to Thunder Canyon tonight. At least in the cabin they'd be warm and dry. They'd brought enough food to last them a week.

Brad thought about the cell phone clipped to his belt. What were the chances he could still get a signal out here?

The car's tires swished through the slushy snow and water on the bridge.

As Brad covered the half mile, then veered off the road to take the lane to the cabin, he could tell that here the two or three inches of new powder that had fallen tonight covered patches of old snow that still hadn't melted.

The sedan's tires churned beneath them, and he couldn't make any more headway up the incline. "This is it. Why don't you stay in the car while I get the supplies unloaded. You'll be warm and—"

"I'm coming with you."

"Emily…"

"I'm not the damsel-in-distress type, Brad."

After he switched on the inside light, his appraisal of her was quick, from her off-white sweater to her flat tan leather shoes. "I may have to carry *you* inside, as well as the supplies. How far do you think you're going to get in those shoes?"

When she looked him over, from his jean jacket to his black boots, she mumbled, "I have sneakers in my suitcase."

"Good. You'll need them. Do you want me to get them out now?"

She shook her head. When she did, he couldn't help but follow the sway of her dark hair along her cheeks. He couldn't help but think how silky it looked and how he'd love to feel its softness in his hands.

"I'll keep the sneakers dry for tomorrow," she responded quietly. "Let's just get inside."

Blocking thoughts of touching Emily out of his head, realizing she was as stubborn as he was, he didn't argue with her. If she wanted wet feet, that was her choice.

As Brad exited the car, snow fell on his head and shoulders. He took in a couple of lungfuls of cold night air, surveyed the pines not far from the cabin illuminated by the car's headlights and realized he was glad he was here. He'd only be in Montana a few days, but already he was relieved he was away from the city...away from his father...away from Suzette Brouchard and a situation he couldn't resolve until the lab results came in.

Out here, all of that seemed very far away.

After he rounded the car to open the trunk, Emily appeared beside him. He'd loaded batteries into the flashlight after he'd bought it and now he used it to guide his key into the lock on the trunk. When it popped open, he shone the beam inside.

Emily reached for her suitcase, but his hand covered hers. "I'll get that."

His skin meeting hers sent an electric jolt to his system. When his gaze collided with hers, he saw she was as affected by the result of their contact as he was. Her expression was startled, her eyes wide with man-woman awareness. Snow was settling in her hair, falling onto her long, dark lashes unenhanced by mascara. They didn't need to be enhanced.

When she shivered, he ordered gruffly, "Just grab a bag with groceries. I'll take care of the rest."

Ignoring his instructions, she hung her camera bag around her neck, then picked up two bags and started the ten-yard trek to the cabin.

Brad swore softly, shook his head and decided the next few days were going to be damn interesting. For the past six months Emily Stanton had played the part of a dependable secretary who kept her opinions to herself. Now he realized there was a woman behind that facade—a woman with spirit and a mind of her own.

The rustic-looking log cabin didn't have a porch, simply two snow-covered redwood steps leading to the door.

Watching Emily as her small feet sank into the snow, Brad followed her. When the sole of her leather shoe sank onto the first step, her foot slipped. He realized he'd been expecting that to happen.

Dropping the suitcases, his arms went around her and the grocery bags to prevent her and their supplies from tumbling into the snow. Her shoulder brushed his chest as he caught her, and his nose grazed her hair— hair that smelled like flowers!

As she looked up at him, their faces were very close. Their white breaths in the cold air mingled as she said, "I'm fine," and he murmured, "I've got you."

For a long, silent winter moment, everything went still. Their body heat seemed to create a cocoon of warmth diametrically opposed to the elements surrounding them. With the headlights of the car shining toward the cabin, he could see her expression in the shadows. It was questioning now—surprised and even a little curious. He was curious, too, about the vibrations humming between them, the chemistry that had seemed to spring up out of nowhere yesterday outside his office. Snowflakes landed on Emily's bangs, on his nose. If he bent his head, their lips would brush. If he turned her to face him…

A gust of wind buffeted them.

He had to get a grip. This wasn't a fun getaway for two. They were in Thunder Canyon to work and nothing else. He and Emily weren't from the same world. In many ways she was very much like his ex-fiancée, Robin. She came from a blue-collar family, hadn't known many advantages and was trying to make the best of her circumstances. Robin had made the best of her circumstances by accepting his father's check and bailing out of Brad's life.

Years later, he knew he should never have gone after her. He should never have heard her say she had feelings for him but wanted the good life *now*. His father's money had given her freedom, and she wanted to experience it alone.

The good life. Freedom. He had both, but lately he'd felt more restless than satisfied or happy.

Releasing Emily, he said, "We're getting wet."

As another gust of wind and snow brushed across the front of the cabin, Brad used the key Caleb had given him, pushed the door open and stepped inside.

Emily watched Brad enter like a man on a mission. She could hardly keep her teeth from chattering now, but for those few moments when Brad had held her she'd been as warm as toast.

He hadn't held her. He'd caught her. And if she hadn't seen the desire in his eyes to kiss her…

She simply hadn't. Her imagination was working way past overtime.

Suddenly she realized Brad had probably gone into the cabin ahead of her to search for creatures. Were there bears in Montana?

She'd seen those movies where animals in the wild had broken through windows and played havoc inside a vacationer's paradise.

This was not her idea of a vacation. A vacation destination for her would be a sunny beach on an island, swimming to her heart's content, dancing under the stars.

With whom?

Shaking disturbing visions of Brad from her mental images, she followed the glow of Brad's flashlight as he found the light switch.

The switch controlled the overhead light in the kitchen, and she took in the place where they'd be spending the night. They'd stepped into a living room with a wood floor, Native American patterned rugs, a hunter-green tweedy sofa and a tan leather club chair with a buffalo painted on its cushion. The log walls were devoid of decoration, but a bookshelf sat against one wall across from the club chair. The sofa faced the fireplace that was small but beautiful with its stone hearth and chimney.

Peering straight through the living room, she saw the small kitchen had an oven, burners and a compact refrigerator. To her left, she tried to see into the darkness of the bedroom, but she wasn't able to. She supposed the bathroom was in there.

Finding the thermostat on the wall, Brad went to it and heat clicked on. "I'll get the rest of the supplies. Don't even think about trying to help me," he said with a stern look. "Get warm."

For some reason, when he looked at her, she got *very* warm. But she'd never admit *that*.

Taking her suitcase from the floor, he carried it to the bedroom. She saw him turn on a small lamp and then he set her valise on the bed.

"You can sleep in there tonight," he said, emerging from the bedroom. "I'll take the sofa."

In the office setting, Emily hadn't glimpsed Brad's chivalrous side, though he did always open doors for her. She was a bit surprised by it.

When Brad opened the door to return outside, she heard the wind howl. He was going to freeze until he brought everything in. She knew he was probably used to fine brandy, but tonight maybe he'd appreciate hot chocolate.

As Brad brought in the last of the bags of supplies and placed them on the wrought-iron-and-glass kitchen table, he began un-packing them. After storing the cookies in an upper cabinet, he put milk and juice into the refrigerator. Emily couldn't help but watch his every move.

"What?" he asked when he caught her interest.

She felt color rise to her cheeks. She'd been admiring his height, his broad shoulders, his adaptability to the situation. Brad Vaughn had to be used to maid service, but he was putting his groceries away. "Nothing."

"What were you thinking, Emily?" His gaze pinned her to the spot, and she knew he wasn't going to let her evade him. Brad didn't let anybody evade him.

Choosing her words carefully, she selected the ones that were most diplomatic. "I was just surprised you were putting away the supplies."

Like a panther cornering its prey, Brad took a few steps closer to her. "Surprised?"

"Guys don't usually think about things like that."

To her relief, he didn't seem angry. "Guys? Meaning any guy in particular?"

His closeness unnerved her, and she quietly unscrambled her thoughts. "My brother, for instance. You'd think with three sisters and a mom he would have learned to pick up after himself after all these years. But even his wife says he's impossible."

Instead of focusing on her brother, Brad asked, "Did your parents divorce?"

"No. Dad died when I was ten. An aneurysm he never knew he had burst."

"I'm sorry. You said you have a brother and sisters?"

"Eric's two years older than I am. Lizbeth and Elaine are younger. What about you? Brothers and sisters?"

Brad shook his head. As the wind rattled the windowpane, he still studied her closely. "It must have been hard for your mom to raise you on her own."

"It was. We all had part-time jobs as soon as we could."

When he reached out and slid his hand down the back of her hair, she closed her eyes, amazed by the sensations coursing through her.

"It's still damp," he murmured.

"It will dry," she responded, opening her eyes again, gazing into his brown ones, suddenly wanting to feel his lips on hers more than anything else she'd ever wanted.

The windowpane rattled again, and she couldn't believe she was even thinking such a thought. Gathering her wits about her, she turned away from him and switched off the burner on the stove. "I'll have hot chocolate ready in a minute, and then we can think about supper."

"If we can agree on what to eat." His voice was a bit husky. "Your taste and mine seem to run in different directions."

"I don't eat a lot of meat," she admitted. "But if you want to pan fry that steak, I can make a huge salad—"

All at once, there was sudden and complete darkness and an all-encompassing silence. Then the wind whooshed against the cabin once more and the whole building seemed to quake.

"Damn," she heard Brad mutter. "Where's my flashlight?"

"I have a penlight on my key chain."

"But you'd have to find your key chain," he said in a wry tone.

In the pitch blackness she knew it would be hard to find anything. As afraid as she was in their present situation, Emily was concerned that if she moved she'd bump into Brad, and that seemed even more dangerous than standing in darkness in a strange place. So she stayed put, trying to remember where she'd dropped her purse. She thought it was on the buffalo chair, but she wasn't sure.

She heard Brad moving around, shifting bags on the table. Finally he announced, "Got it." A moment later, a beam of light streaked to where she was standing.

"I'm fine, but what are we going to do? Without the power, we don't have any heat."

"Slow down, Emily. We've got a fireplace. There's wood on the hearth and probably more out back. I think I spotted an oil lantern over on those bookshelves."

Dipping his hand into one of their bags, he produced matches. After he found the lantern, he lit it. The light vanquished some of the darkness in the living room area.

"There's a can of lantern oil here, but we should still probably conserve it. Why don't you make that hot chocolate while I go out and check the wood supply."

"Why check it? If we already have some here—"

"I have to see how much we have. We may have to make it last."

"Only one night." While he aimed the flashlight at the floor, she couldn't see his face in the shadows. "Brad? It's only going to be one night, isn't it?"

"Let's just take things as they come."

"What aren't you telling me? We can't get snowed in here for days, can we?"

"I doubt that, but I don't want to run out of wood, either."

"From what I could see, there were trees everywhere."

"There are. But even if I had an ax, everything's wet. Green wood smokes. I'm hoping there's a supply of covered logs out back. Make the hot chocolate."

He was keeping something from her—she knew he was—and she wasn't going to plead with him to tell her. She wouldn't plead with a man for anything.

Five minutes later, when Brad returned from checking the wood pile, his face looked grim.

Emily panicked. "What?"

He'd carried in a few logs and now he deposited them on the hearth. "This is it."

She was shivering again. She'd taken off her sweater because it was damp from the snow. The temperature in the cabin was only a little warmer than when they'd arrived. Her slacks were still wet and her stockings, too.

Shrugging out of his jacket, he hung it over a kitchen chair. He was wearing a western-cut, blue plaid shirt, and the truth was, he looked as if he belonged in Montana. *She* obviously didn't. Brad Vaughn was sexy enough in the suits he usually wore, but in jeans and a snap-button shirt…

She swallowed hard.

"What do you want to do first? Drink the hot chocolate or change your clothes?" He looked down at her slacks, which were wrinkled against her ankles. "You've got to get out of the wet clothes so you can warm up. I hope you brought something comfortable."

At the last minute, she'd thrown in a pair of sweats. "I did, but I don't really have anything warm."

"I've got to get the fire going. Once I do that, we'll raid the closets and drawers and see what we can find. We'll both have to sleep in here tonight by the fire to keep warm."

Her gaze automatically slanted to the sofa.

"You can have that," he said generously. "I'll make a bedroll on the floor."

"That'll be hard."

"I've camped out before. I'll be fine. If it gets too uncomfortable, I can always try the buffalo chair. I can usually sleep anywhere."

Sleeping brought to mind beds. Beds brought to mind what men and women did in beds. Pushing away visions of her and Brad in a bed, she remembered the article in the newspaper yesterday morning. She remembered Suzette Brouchard and the claim that Brad was her baby's father. She remembered Brad's rich-bachelor lifestyle.

"Go on," he said with a nod. "Take your hot chocolate with you. Drink it while it's warm."

"We won't be able to make steak for supper."

"We're not going to starve. We have plenty of food and we've got the Sterno burners. Relax, Emily. You're going to get gray hair if you keep worrying about everything."

Suddenly the whole situation—Montana, the snow, being cooped up with Brad Vaughn in the cabin—got to be too overwhelming.

As she straightened her shoulders and lifted her chin, she said, "Maybe I've never been to Montana and maybe I've never gone camping, but you don't have to treat me like a child."

Picking up her mug of hot chocolate, she tried not to let it slosh over her hand as she made her escape into the bedroom.

It would have been a good exit, but then Brad called to her. "Emily, you're going to need this."

When she turned, he held out the flashlight to her. "I can use the oil lamp. You won't be able to see in the bedroom."

Did she spot amusement in his eyes? Was that an almost smile at the corner of his lips?

Grabbing the flashlight, she mumbled, "Thank you," and headed for the dark room.

After she pushed the door shut, she hated the fact that tears pricked in her eyes. The attraction to Brad Vaughn that had plagued her ever since she'd started working at Vaughn Associates had been buried with a lot of effort. But this trip was bringing it to the surface, and she didn't want it. She didn't need it. As soon as Lizbeth graduated from college at the end of May, she was going to earn her own degree. Then she could become more than a secretary. She could become anything she wanted—except maybe the kind of woman Brad Vaughn dated.

That doesn't matter, she chastised herself.

After she fiddled with the flashlight, unpacked her suitcase and found the clothes she wanted, she changed, not anxious to go back into the fray with Brad. The violet sweats had been a Christmas gift from her sisters. They were comfortable, as were the crew socks she pulled onto her feet. With her wet clothes off, the room was still cold but she didn't feel quite as chilled.

Sniffing, she caught the scent of burning wood. She'd lived in an apartment all her life and had never been in a house with a fireplace. That more than anything else urged her to open the bedroom door and go back out into dangerous territory.

But when she stepped into the living room, she froze.

Brad was standing in front of the fire, pulling a pair of jeans from his suitcase on the sofa.

He was stark naked!

Chapter Three

In spite of herself, Emily couldn't look away. Brad was magnificent with the firelight flickering over his skin, shadows playing in intimate places. Stunned and absolutely speechless, she noticed that with no shirt to hide his muscles, Brad's shoulders seemed twice as broad. His chest hair was black and curly, and as she followed it down—

Either she made a sound or he sensed her presence. Rather than looking embarrassed, though, he tossed her a grin, obviously unashamed of his body.

She swiveled around, ready to run back to the bedroom, when she heard the rustle of jeans, the clank of a buckle and the quick rasp of a zipper.

"You can turn around now. I didn't expect you to come out so quickly. Women usually take a lot longer than that to change their clothes."

Maybe the women *he* dated.

Her hand went to her hair. She hadn't even taken time to brush it after she'd slipped on the violet top that went with her pants. "I guess I'm not your typical woman," she responded blithely.

Though her cheeks still felt as if they were on fire, looking straight ahead, she went to the kitchen, trying to pretend seeing him naked hadn't affected her at all. Although he'd pulled on jeans, the snap above his fly was still undone, his belt buckle was unfastened and he was shirtless.

"So what's for supper?" she asked him, her heart still racing as she kept her gaze away from his bare skin.

After he pulled on socks, he rummaged in his suitcase to find a flannel shirt. "Since we had the hot chocolate and we have a good fire, why don't we go with peanut butter sandwiches and a can of fruit for tonight. In the morning we can use the Sterno and try to cook eggs."

She knew he'd bought more than one Sterno unit. Nevertheless, she still had the feeling Brad was keeping something from her. Maybe he was concerned the snow would fall more heavily during the night and they wouldn't be able to dig themselves out.

"Peanut butter's good, but *you* can have the can of fruit. I'll eat an apple."

"A purist," he teased with a smile that almost made her toes curl.

"With some things," she tossed over her shoulder.

The kitchen was cold and getting colder. Only the living room held warmth, because of the fire. "I guess we could eat on the sofa."

"If you want to stay warm."

With him beside her on the sofa, she had the feeling she'd be plenty warm. While she made the peanut butter sandwiches—two for him, one for her—he popped the top on the can of fruit and then hunted in the cupboard for the cookies he'd stowed there. He'd let his shirt hang out over his jeans, and she had the disturbing urge to slip her hands under it and touch his bare skin.

What in the world was happening to her?

With a quick twist of her wrist, she closed the jar of peanut butter. "You never did tell me how you learned to clean up after yourself."

Leaning against the counter, holding the bag of cookies, he casually crossed one foot over the other. "No, I didn't."

The sound of his voice was unusual. "Does that mean you're *not* going to tell me?"

"You're different here than you are in the office."

If that was his way of not answering her question, it wouldn't work. She wasn't going to let him turn the tables on her. "And *you're* changing the subject."

The oil lamp on the kitchen table flickered, as if a sudden draft had given it renewed life. Its light was reflected in Brad's eyes. He seemed to stare at the flame for a few seconds before his gaze finally met hers. "Kids pick up habits out of necessity."

The statement seemed incongruous with his background. It was well known that Phillip Vaughn had come from money, even if he hadn't been successful in his own right. As a boy, Brad should have had every advantage, as well as a maid picking up after him.

Uncrossing his ankles, the casual pose

forgotten, Brad set the cookies on the counter as if he'd suddenly lost his appetite for them.

As she thought about his statement, she said softly, "I know what you mean. After Dad died, Mom was scattered. Since Eric was the oldest and a boy, she looked to him to do some of the things Dad had done—everything from taking out the garbage to helping sort through her finances. Lizbeth, Elaine and I had to pretty much fend for ourselves. Since I was the oldest of the three of us, I took care of them and also took over a lot of the household chores. Mom had to work longer hours to make ends meet."

"Did you resent it?"

"I'd like to say I didn't, but sometimes I did when my friends could do things I couldn't. But most of the time I just felt needed. I learned how to manage time, leftovers in the refrigerator, even the girls' activities. What about you? Did you resent what you had to learn?"

"My situation was different from yours."

Waiting, she hoped patience would encourage Brad to go on. It did.

"My parents divorced when I was twelve. I lived with my mother during the school week, and on weekends I lived with my dad in the house where I'd grown up. In the beginning I would forget a schoolbook at one place, a favorite toy at another. I couldn't depend on anyone to know exactly what I needed except for me. It became important for me to find a place for everything—then I could lay a hand on it at a moment's notice."

"That must have been so hard having two homes but not a real home." Brad must have constantly felt as if he were being pulled in two directions.

He shrugged. "I got used to it, but no child should have to."

Picking up the two paper plates with the sandwiches, he nodded toward the sofa. "Come on. Let's eat."

In the living room Brad set the plates on the wrought-iron-and-glass coffee table in front of the sofa. He'd brought along a can of soda with the cookies, and Emily had picked up a bottle of water.

Instead of sitting, Brad moved the coffee table to the side and pushed the sofa closer to the fire. "If you're cold, I could pull a blanket off the bed."

She curled in a corner of the sofa closest to the fire. "I'm okay for now."

When Brad sat beside Emily, there was half a sofa cushion between them, and it seemed like no space at all. They made polite conversation as they ate, and Emily began to relax. To her surprise, Brad was easy to talk to as she explained she'd like to go to college. He drew her out about courses she was interested in. When she asked him about his years on Wall Street, he told her stories that made her laugh.

As the fire burned lower, the windowpanes stopped rattling, and she hoped the storm was over.

Brad had opened the pack of chocolate cookies and now he held it out to her. "Want one?"

Her apple had disappeared after her peanut butter sandwich. The chocolate-covered cookie with marshmallow in the center *did* look good. Pulling one from the bag, she took a bite. Then she closed her eyes and savored it.

Brad's voice was low and deep as he said, "There are a lot more. You don't have to spend so much time on that one."

After she opened her eyes, she realized he'd been watching her. She'd been enjoying the cookie as if it were the most sensual experience on earth, and he'd apparently seen that. He'd apparently *liked* seeing that.

When he looked at her as if she were one of those chocolate cookies, her breath almost stopped. For two years she'd watched Brad from afar, wondering what he was like. Six months ago, when he'd given her the job as his personal secretary, she'd told herself any attraction she felt had to be swept under a rug. She'd warned herself against feeling anything for him. Her relationship with Warner Bradshaw should have taught her that men like Brad, men like Warner, thought they ruled the world.

But tonight she'd seen a different side to Brad and she liked it. Her thoughts slipped back to seeing him naked by the firelight, and she knew more than anything in the world that this moment she wanted him to kiss her. She'd shifted from her corner of the couch in the course of their conversation and now her knee practically brushed his.

"Emily." Low and husky, his voice fell over her as his gaze roamed her face.

Her mouth went dry as she managed a small, "What?"

Moving closer to her, his thumb stroked over her upper lip. "Chocolate crumbs."

When her hand went to her lips, it was caught by his. "Since yesterday," he began, "there's been a buzz between us. Do you feel it?"

She could only nod.

He leaned even closer. "I'm going to kiss you."

It was a declaration of intent, and she realized why he'd made it. She could move away. She could run to the bedroom and shut the door. She could pretend she wanted another chocolate cookie more than his kiss. But that wouldn't be true.

For months she'd wanted to run her fingers through his hair. For months she'd seen his beard shadow at the end of the day and wondered what it would feel like against her cheek. His stubble now made him look even sexier than usual, if that was possible.

As his hand came up to cup her cheek, she kept perfectly still, afraid she'd break the spell.

His long, warm fingers slid into her hair as he brought her face closer to his.

The fire crackled in the hearth as a different fire that had lain dormant for months came to life inside of her. When Brad's lips covered hers, tiny rockets exploded all

through her body and she wanted one thing—
to experience more.

Brad's tongue slipped inside her mouth,
and after a few moments of pure erotic pleasure, he pulled back. He was breathing rag-
gedly and so was she as he smiled at her.
"You taste like peanut butter and chocolate."

She couldn't speak because the kiss had
been too short—an appetizer when she
wanted the whole meal. That must have
shown in her eyes.

With a groan, his head bent to hers again,
and this time there was no holding back as
he let his hunger show.

Brad Vaughn not only looked sexy, he *was*
sexy. She'd never experienced anything like
his kiss. It was intense and demanding and
seductive. Her hand went to the nape of his
neck and she inhaled his scent. She inhaled
Brad.

The longer they kissed, the more the
strokes of his tongue inflamed her. The longer they kissed, the more her thoughts scattered. The longer they kissed, the more she
forgot about everything but Brad.

As he laid her back on the sofa, she em-
braced him, eager to stroke his back, eager
to lift his shirt and feel his hot skin.

At her touch, he shuddered, then he stilled and broke the kiss. Propped on his forearms, he stared down at her. "Do you know what you're doing?"

The question brought Emily back to the real world, and that wasn't the cabin where they were stranded. He brought her back to her life in Chicago and who she was and who he was. Then she remembered the pain when Warner had left and she remembered the devastation when she'd lost her baby. For goodness' sake, Brad had been accused of fathering a woman's child! Didn't that show her the writing on the wall?

When she tried to scramble to a sitting position, he lifted himself off her and sat on the sofa. "That's what I thought," he muttered.

Although she was upset, flustered and still longing for more of his kisses, she asked indignantly, "What does *that* mean?"

He ran his hand over his face. "Nothing. We both just got caught up in the moment."

But she couldn't let it go. She had a feeling he was making comparisons and she didn't like it. "I guess I've had a lot fewer of those moments than you have." It was meant to be a stab at his lifestyle, but it wasn't a very good one.

"I know."

His attitude fired her anger because she wasn't as naive as he thought. "You don't know everything."

"No, I don't. If I knew everything, I wouldn't have asked you to come along."

That stung, and she couldn't help the quick tears that came to her eyes. Not wanting him to see, she turned away from him, picked up the empty paper plates and announced, "I'm going to get ready for bed."

"I'll try to get some water from the pump. You won't be able to flush the toilet without it."

How did he know all of these things?

She hated depending on his know-how, on his survival skills, but she had no choice. She just knew she was going to keep her distance from him until they got back to Thunder Canyon and civilization. Until they got back to Chicago, where everything would be ordinary again.

When Brad awakened the following morning, sun streamed in the cabin windows. The fire had gone out and the rooms were cold. Immediately he noticed Emily was still asleep, almost invisible cuddled inside the two blankets she'd wrapped around herself.

They'd gone to sleep in stony silence, and that had been his fault. He shouldn't have kissed her. He shouldn't have even *thought* about kissing her.

Still troubled by feelings he didn't understand, troubled by the effects of that kiss, he drew back his blankets and sat up. Fortunately he'd found extra covers in the closet, along with a sheepskin jacket and a down parka. Brad wondered if they belonged to Caleb or whoever had lived here before. It didn't matter. He was just glad someone had left them.

He'd slept in his clothes last night, in deference to Emily, not wanting a repeat of what had happened last evening when she'd caught him naked. He'd try to play it low-key, but the way her eyes had roved over him had unsettled him, raised his temperature and made him wonder what it was about this woman that suddenly got to him.

When he threw back the covers and stood, Emily's head popped up from under her blankets. "Where are you going?" She was sleep-tousled, and her voice was husky from awakening quickly.

Trying for a casual tone, he answered with, "After I brush my teeth, I'm going to try to dig us out. I know it's cold in here, but I think we should wait until I come back in to light the fire."

"But if we're leaving today—"

That's what she wanted and so did he, but he didn't think it was going to happen. "Last night when I brought in the bucket of water, we'd already gotten about four to six inches of snow. I'm not sure that car can handle it."

She looked totally crestfallen.

"As I said, I'm going out to assess the damage."

Quickly sitting up, she declared, "I'm going with you."

"Emily, there's no need."

"We're stranded here together, Brad. I'm going to do my part."

By now he'd realized she had a very stubborn streak. "Fine. You can wear that parka we found. It should keep you warm."

Before she could argue with him about that, he headed for the bathroom.

As they stepped outside fifteen minutes later, the sun gleaming off the snow almost blinded them. Emily held her hand to her forehead like a visor and turned in slow circles, scanning all of it. "I can't believe anyone would want a cabin out here. It's so deserted." The parka seemed to swallow her up, and she looked adorable.

"It's isolated, but there could be a neighbor over the next rise. There's plenty of creatures, too, if you look for them. I don't think I've ever been anyplace more...serene. Listen," he advised her.

When she did, a puzzled expression came over her face. "I don't hear anything."

"That's the point. Where else can you hear silence like this?"

Her gaze met his, and the powerful connection he'd felt last night when he was kissing her seemed to be there again. But then she broke eye contact and glanced at the car. It was snow-covered, and her expression fell.

"I found a shovel and broom out back last night. I'll get them, then see if we can move the car." But he doubted that they'd be able to move it very far.

She motioned to the sun, whose rays were a welcome relief from the cold inside the cabin. "Maybe it will melt it all."

"Maybe it will," he agreed, yet he knew snowmelt from the mountains could cause more problems. It was the reason the creek was already running full.

For the next half hour he shoveled around the tires of the car, while Emily used the broom to brush the snow from the hood and the trunk, then returned to the cabin for her camera. He was aware of her shooting photos of the scenery.

After he'd also shoveled the snow away from around the car, he gazed down the half mile that led to the bridge.

Taking the car keys from his pocket, he said, "I'm going to see how far I can get."

Before he could stop her, she'd climbed in the passenger side.

"Afraid I'll leave you behind?" he asked with a chuckle.

"I'm not taking any chances."

Although the remark might have been joking, Brad sensed Emily didn't trust him. He'd sensed that in the wall she kept around herself since she'd become his secretary. Last night that wall had slipped, but now she was evidently sorry about that.

After a cough and a sputter, the car started up. But as soon as Brad left the area he'd shoveled, he was spinning his tires. When he glanced at Emily, he saw her expression—it was near panic. "This obviously isn't going to work. We'll have to try something else."

"What else is there to try? We're stuck."

Their contact last night made it easy to lay a comforting hand on her arm. "Caleb knows we're here. He'll get us out if we can't manage to get ourselves out."

Suddenly her face brightened. "You have a cell phone, don't you?"

"I tried it last night. I couldn't get a signal up here in the mountains. This morning when I turned it on, the battery had run down."

Her expression looked so forlorn, he joked, "I'll have to give you an even bigger bonus after this trip."

Her large green eyes went wider. "Why? Because of that kiss last night?"

He knew she thought he was a ladies' man, but the idea that he'd up her bonus because of the kiss really irked him. "It was more than one kiss, and you were as involved as I was. But, no, that's not the reason I'll give you combat pay. I think you deserve overtime for being stranded where you obviously don't want to be."

Then he exited the car before he gave in to the temptation to kiss her again.

Inside the cabin once more, Brad lit the fire so they could warm up. It was almost noon, and he decided to make scrambled eggs on the Sterno burner. Emily was skeptical, and it took a while, but eventually they sat down to a lunch of scrambled eggs and buttered bread. As she had the night before, she added fruit to her meal while he finished a candy bar and thought about their options. There weren't a lot of them, and he considered his comment to her this morning. There *could* be a neighbor just over the rise—a neighbor with a four-wheel-drive vehicle. Just as Caleb had purchased this cabin during the gold-rush siege, other people had also discovered Thunder Canyon and the surrounding area. He'd heard a movie star had even purchased a ranch near Caleb's new ski-resort project.

The summer Brad had spent in Montana with his friend James, he'd learned survival skills. He knew how to tell direction from the angle of the sun, the growth on the trees, landmarks he would designate.

Emily was trying to scrub the frying pan with water from the bucket and soap she'd found under the sink. She hadn't said much since they'd returned to the cabin, and he was sorry he'd been so gruff before. He didn't want to hurt her feelings. He didn't want to take advantage of her.

He didn't want to be attracted to her.

That more than anything made him say, "I'm going to go exploring this afternoon. Maybe I can find somebody who lives closer than we think."

"I'll go with you."

"No. I can go a lot faster without you and I want to get some ground covered." He could see the sun had slipped behind a cloud. In the mountains, the weather could change from minute to minute.

In a gentler tone he suggested, "You stay here, stay warm, keep the home fires burning. Though if you can help it, try not to use more than one log, okay?"

"Brad, this isn't a good idea." She looked downright worried.

He stood and went to the kitchen. "Are you afraid to stay here alone?"

"No! Well, yes," she finally admitted. "And I don't like the idea of you out there trekking in the cold and snow."

Taking her by the shoulders, he looked deep into her eyes. "I know what I'm doing, Emily. I spent a summer in Montana with a friend. We went backpacking for three weeks. What I didn't learn then, I've learned since on other backpacking trips. So you don't have to worry."

"I *will* worry," she said honestly, and he wondered how long it had been since somebody actually worried about him. That thought unsettled him just as Emily herself unsettled him. He hated to admit it, but for the past two days, being around her had made his life seem less empty. She soothed his spirit somehow, and he wasn't as restless.

The urge to touch her, the urge to kiss her again, was too much of a temptation. Stepping away from her, he said, "I'm going to wear the parka. It's warmer. Don't go outside unless you absolutely have to. Understand?"

"All right," she agreed.

Reaching to the counter for one of her PowerBars, he winked. "I'll take this along in case I get hungry."

When she gave him a small smile, he knew he had to leave—now. Too much about Emily Stanton was getting under his skin. A walk in the snow was just what he needed.

For the first hour Brad was gone, Emily did just fine—except for watching him walk away and disappear behind some pine trees. That's when her stomach sank. Every fifteen minutes she went to the window and peered out, wishing he'd stayed in the cabin with her. Finally settling on the sofa, she read a magazine she'd packed in her suitcase. Then, still restless, she studied the titles of the books on the bookshelf and drank a can of juice.

But during the second hour the sky turned gray, the clouds seemed even more forbidding and the damp cold in the cabin seemed even damper without Brad. A tight knot formed in her stomach. He'd left at one, and by two-thirty she was worried sick. What if he'd slipped and fallen? What if he'd frozen to death? What if—

She couldn't stay cooped up. The fire had almost burned out, and she didn't know whether to add another log or not. The sheepskin coat Brad had worn that morning hung over a kitchen chair. Slipping it on, she thought she could smell him. She remembered how he'd looked in it—like a rugged outdoorsman. It was warm, and before she considered his warning to stay inside, she added her sweater under the coat, turned up the collar and went outside.

Snow was falling lightly and she had no idea what she was going to do. She just knew she couldn't sit still any longer.

Brad's footsteps were visible from the back of the cabin in a line that seemed to lead very far away. Trying to keep her sneakers from getting too wet, she stepped into each one of his prints, though it was a stretch. His legs were much longer than hers. Everything about him was so distinctly male. She couldn't erase the picture of him naked. She couldn't dismiss the erotic sensuality of his kiss.

With each step she took, the snow fell a little more heavily and wind began to blow. She had to turn back.

Gazing into the distance, she stared at the pine trees, wishing she could see through them. She stared so hard her eyes blurred and then she saw something...someone. At first she believed it was her imagination or a wishful mirage that she had conjured up. But then she recognized the green down parka, the fur-lined hood. He was walking in a straight line toward her and she didn't move. Not until he was about ten feet away.

Then she ran to him and threw her arms around his neck. "Oh, I'm so glad you're okay. I was so worried. You didn't come back and you didn't come back...."

The hood came down over his eyes and his face, but now he brushed it back and it fell away. He was looking down at her with hunger in his eyes and the desire she'd glimpsed there last night. Now it seemed to flame even brighter. "I'm back. I'm fine. Come on, let's get you into the cabin."

But neither of them moved, and she felt tears come to her eyes. "I was afraid you'd been hurt."

Although he'd told her he was fine, that wasn't enough. Her arms hooked around his neck, and he held her. Their breath mingled as he lowered his lips to hers.

The kiss was so hot she forgot it was snowing. The kiss was so desire filled her head swam. One minute she was standing there kissing him and the next he'd scooped her up into his arms and he was kissing her. Then he carried her to the cabin in much less time than it had taken her to walk in his footsteps.

Once inside, he kissed her all over again. Their lips melded, their tongues tangled and their need for each other seemed to explode out of control.

Carrying her to the bedroll, he set her down

there and knelt down beside her. "I want you, Emily."

"I want you, too." Making love with Brad had been in her dreams for months. Now they were alone together, needing each other. Couldn't she make at least part of her dream come true?

Unzipping his parka, he tossed it onto the floor beside him. She slipped off her coat and sweater and looked up at him with all the anxiety of the past hour and a half. "I was so worried about you."

"I worried about you, too, at the cabin alone. But I wanted to try to get us out."

He had been out hiking for her.

When she reached up to him, he bent down to her. This time the kissing was even more urgent. After he undressed her, he pulled a blanket over her. Seconds later he was undressed, too, slipping under the blanket with her. As he took her into his arms, she played her hand across his chest, loving the feel of his hair, loving the feel of *him*.

Any cold that had lingered from the outdoors dissipated in the heat of their passion as his legs tangled with hers. When his hand caressed her breast, she moaned with such pleasure that she didn't recognize herself.

Every place he touched seemed doubly sensitized. Every kiss he planted on her lips, her neck and her navel made her sigh his name.

"What do you want, Emily?" he asked, finally stretching out on top of her, finally giving her some of the satisfaction she craved.

"I want *you*. I want you inside me."

He gave her what she wanted. The first thrust almost took her over the edge, but then he stilled, savoring their fit.

Brad had played her body to a fever pitch, and now it was demanding release. She couldn't stay still. When she contracted around him, he groaned. Raising her knees, she hugged his thighs and severed the thread of his self-restraint. Thrusting deeper and harder, he set a rhythm that became hers. She rocked with him until he slipped one hand between them and ignited her climax. The moment seemed to go on and on forever, and he kissed her until his release came. When he shuddered, she held him tight, never wanting to let him go.

But minutes later, as Brad pushed himself up on his forearms, then rolled off of her, she caught a glimpse of his face and knew she had to let him go.

As he lay back staring up at the ceiling, shame and regret and hurt filled her. And before he said something she knew she wouldn't want to hear, she asked accusingly, "Is this the way it happened with Suzette?"

Chapter Four

Brad's face had been somber but now his jaw set and he looked angry. "I have *never* had sex with a woman before without protection."

She found herself wanting to believe him…wanting to believe him with all her heart. She'd like to believe he'd wanted her as much as she'd wanted him and absolutely nothing else had mattered. Maybe at the moment she had mattered to him, but she was afraid it had been just for the moment.

"I can't believe I was that stupid." She sat up and dropped her head into her hands on her knees.

When she'd been seeing Warner, she'd been on the pill and she hadn't missed a day. But somehow she'd made it into that one-percent-failure ratio and had gotten pregnant. This time, however, if she got pregnant, it would be her own fault.

Sitting up beside her, Brad said gently, "If you get pregnant, you won't have to go through it alone."

How many men had told women that? She remembered Warner saying a kid wasn't in his plans. Brad probably meant he'd give her money, just as he'd wanted to give her an extra bonus. That's the last thing she even wanted to consider. "You mean you'd stick by me like you stuck by Suzette?"

"I am *not* the father of Suzette Brouchard's child."

"Then why did she make the accusation?"

"It really doesn't matter, does it, Emily? Because you're dead set on not believing me anyway. I don't know what I've ever done to you that you think I'd treat you shabbily or take advantage of you."

"You've never done anything to me," she admitted honestly. "But I've seen pictures of the women you date. I read the tidbits in the gossip columns. I pass personal calls on to you. Your relationships don't last much longer than a thunderstorm."

When he studied her face, she suspected an angry retort, but he didn't give her one. "You think what you want to think."

Then he was on his feet and pulling on his jeans. "That log isn't going to get us through the night. I'm going to try to find some kindling that might be dry enough to burn."

"You shouldn't go back out—"

"This time I won't be gone as long. It was a wasted hike. Tomorrow I'll try hiking *down* the mountain."

Ten minutes ago they'd been locked in the most intimate contact possible between a man and a woman. Now she felt as if they were miles apart. "Thank you for trying."

"No thanks are necessary. We both want to get on with our business in Thunder Canyon."

Stranded at the cabin, she'd forgotten all about the investigation. But at least if they ever got out of here, she'd have something else to think about besides the two of them.

She'd dressed and was putting a salad together for supper, complete with beef jerky and cheese, when Brad returned from outside with kindling. "I'm going to try this before

I burn our last log. But if it begins smoking, we're going to have make do with what we have."

Make do with one log? Just how long would *that* last?

At least they had shelter. They had food and plenty of blankets. They'd be fine.

Yet when Brad's gaze met hers, she didn't feel fine.

As Brad lit the kindling, almost immediately smoke began billowing from the fireplace, as well as up the chimney.

He swore. "That's what I thought, but I had to try it. Come on. Get your coat. Let's go outside for a few minutes until the smoke clears."

Coughing as smoky air penetrated the cabin, she grabbed the sheepskin coat from the chair, shrugged into it and followed him outside.

Snow had stopped falling.

Brad glanced up at the sky. "It looks as if the weather's going to break."

"I wonder why Mr. Douglas didn't try to get through to us today. He probably has an SUV or something."

"Even if he tried to get up here with an SUV, he would have had to turn back."

"Why?"

"Because the bridge is flooded from the runoff. We're good and stuck until he figures a way to get us out."

Her expression must have shown her fear and Brad swore again. "I thought you'd be better off knowing the truth of it. But Caleb *will* come get us. A man who could put together the ski-resort deal he just managed should have some kind of contact to get us back over that stream."

Emily was trying to keep from worrying. She was trying to forget what had happened in the cabin not so very long ago. She was trying to keep her feelings for Brad from growing stronger.

Turning away from him, she looked toward a band of snow-topped firs, then stilled. "What's that?" she asked in a low voice.

Brad came over to stand beside her. "That's a bull elk."

"It won't come any closer, will it?"

Brad chuckled. "I don't think he's too keen for our company."

"Maybe he wants food."

"Soon it will be calving season. Maybe he's just looking for some peace and quiet while he can find it."

That observation made her smile.

"Let's see if we can go back in. We don't want to get any colder than we have to. In fact, we should probably warm water for hot chocolate."

"When are we going to burn the last log?"

"Tonight. Before we turn in."

Although that made sense, she was still worried. What if Caleb Douglas didn't rescue them tomorrow?

She wouldn't think about tomorrow. Tonight would be complicated enough.

Emily didn't know what time it was when she awakened in the pitch-black cabin. The log had obviously long died out, and she was freezing. With two blankets doubled on top of her, she was still cold, and no matter what position she curled in, she couldn't generate body heat. She was wearing her sweats. Maybe if she put on more clothes...

In the stillness she assumed Brad was asleep. She didn't hear the rustle of his bedroll or the creak of the floor signaling a change in his position. He'd insisted she keep the flashlight beside her. Now she picked it up from the floor and switched it on with the beam directed at the bedroom. A few minutes later, she'd added a blouse and her sweater but couldn't get her jeans on over the sweatpants. The bedroom was even colder than the living room.

Returning to the sofa, she lay there, her teeth chattering, shivers skipping up and down her body. First she tried curling on her side, then she lay on her back, then she turned toward the sofa cushion cupping her hands around her nose, hoping her breath would warm her face. Finally she turned on her back again.

"Can't sleep?" a deep voice asked.

"I'm cold," she mumbled from beneath the covers. "I put on more clothes, but they're not helping."

There was a long silence until Brad said, "There is another option."

"What? Using the furniture to light the fireplace?"

He chuckled. "Unfortunately the paints and varnishes on the wood furniture would probably smoke like the damp kindling. It's a shame someone loves wrought iron so much. Lodgepole furnishings might have worked."

She didn't know how he could still be in good humor about this. Maybe he wasn't as cold as she was.

"What's the other option?"

"You could sleep with me and we could combine our body heat."

His suggestion generated a definite warmth just thinking about it. "That's not a good idea."

"We could keep our clothes on, Emily. I'm suggesting survival here, not sex."

Was she being a prude? Was she being ridiculous thinking he might want to have sex with her again? Had the union of their bodies meant anything to him?

It had shaken her world and told her in no uncertain terms that she could fall in love with Brad Vaughn.

When she didn't respond, his voice pierced the darkness again. "Think about it."

Then she heard the rustle of covers, as if he'd turned over…as if he were going back to sleep.

What had he said? *I can sleep anywhere.*

She didn't know how much longer she curled on the couch, trying to keep still, re-arranging the covers, pulling her sweater tighter around her. Nothing helped. She just wanted the night to be over. To keep her mind off Brad, she thought about the huge elk they'd seen that afternoon. She heard other noises and didn't know what they were. Was that a coyote howling? Did they have coyotes in Montana?

Finally she gave up. Anything would be better than her mind racing and her body shivering. "Brad?" she asked softly.

"Still can't sleep?"

"No. If I could only stop shivering. Is…is your offer still open?" She felt silly and embarrassed.

It seemed like aeons until he answered, "Sure. Come on down. I'd lay on the sofa with you, but I don't think either of us would have room to breathe."

He was so tall and broad shouldered and muscular. They'd never fit on the sofa.

Switching on the flashlight again so she could see where she was going, she saw him turn onto his side and prop himself on one elbow. "Take off that extra blouse and sweater."

Her gaze met his and her thoughts must have showed.

"I'm not suggesting you undress. Just get rid of those layers. I think you'll be more comfortable. You might want to ditch the sneakers, too."

She didn't know if she was being the biggest fool on the planet as she removed the sweater and blouse and kicked off her sneakers. Then came the real challenge.

Awkwardly she dropped to the bedroll beside him. He'd quadrupled the huge bed quilt underneath him and had doubled the wool blanket on top.

"Do we need my covers from the sofa?"

"Let's try it like this."

Switching off the flashlight, she wasn't sure exactly what position to take.

"Face the sofa," he suggested.

She did that and hovered on the edge of the quilt, as cold as she'd been before.

But then Brad's arms were around her, his chest and stomach were against her back and her backside was curved into his thighs. Seconds later she felt his arousal.

When she would have moved away, he said, "I don't seem to have any control over that, but I'm not going to do anything you don't want me to do."

That was the problem. With his arms around her, with his body pressed close to hers, she wanted to do more than sleep. But making love with Brad Vaughn again would eventually devastate her heart...because *she* thought of it as making love. He thought of

it as having sex. That was a very big difference.

The floor was hard, but for some reason,
with Brad's arms around her, she didn't mind
it.

His warm breath wisped across her ear as
he suggested, "Relax, Emily. Go to sleep.
Hopefully the sun will come out and everything will be better in the morning."

Would everything be better in the morning? She couldn't undo what she'd done. She
couldn't forget about Suzette Brouchard. She
couldn't deny she was falling in love with
Brad, and it was more than a crush. As their
bodies generated the heat he'd predicted, she
felt her thought processes slowing and com-
fort surround her. She felt warm in spite of
the cold. Before she drifted off, however, one
question plagued her. What if she was pregnant with Brad's child?

When Brad suggested Emily sleep with
him, he'd known he was asking for trouble. If
not trouble, a night of discomfort. There was
no way he was touching her again, not sexu-
ally anyway. What they did had blown his
mind. That hour-and-a-half trek must have
frozen his brain as well as his good sense.

His hike had reminded him there should be more to his life than work...work he didn't have a passion for. It had reminded him how his life felt empty sometimes.

So when he'd returned and Emily had flown into his arms, a fire had kick-started. She'd been sweet and soft and honest and utterly guileless, so unlike the women he usually dated. The truth was, he hadn't been thinking at all when they'd started kissing, when they'd started undressing, when they'd come together in a cataclysmic explosion he'd never experienced before.

Afterward, however, conscious thought had hit him like the proverbial ton of bricks. He had never *ever* slept with a woman unprotected before Emily. What was it about her that had made him forget about protection now?

During the early hours of the morning, Emily changed positions. Instead of facing away from him, she turned toward him—unconsciously, he supposed. Now she nestled on his shoulder, throwing one of her legs over his.

He held her loosely in his arms. Loosely, because his self-control was getting hard-pressed. Loosely, because he knew he couldn't be intimate with her a second time. They were wrong for each other, as he'd learned with Robin. If two people didn't grow up with the same backgrounds, there'd be a fatal crash along the road—either a clash of goals or desires or needs.

The problem was, the women he dated *did* have the same backgrounds as he did. Yet he hadn't connected to any of them the way he'd connected to Emily. What did that say about him? What did he have to change?

Although Emily didn't like being stuck here, he did. It was a retreat, a soul easer, and maybe he just needed to take more vacations to remote places.

Emily's hand moved across his chest, and he could feel the path through his sweatshirt as if it were a scalding trail of hot water. When she rubbed her cheek against his shoulder, he almost groaned. Shifting a little, he hoped she'd soon awaken.

After she rubbed her cheek against his shirt a second time, her eyes fluttered open. Their faces were very close together. If he just tilted his head…

He slammed the door shut on that thought.

Self-consciousness dawned in her eyes, and when she realized how she was curled up with him, she scooted away a few inches. "Sorry. I guess I must have rolled over during the night."

Now fully awake, she sat up. Immediately she felt the chill and rubbed her arms.

"Now you can put on that blouse and sweater again." He tried to keep his tone easy. He tried to forget that all he'd wanted to do all night was combine their body heat in a more intimate way.

Scrambling to her feet, she said with determination, "After I brush my teeth, we can get breakfast started. Maybe that will warm us up."

She was babbling fast, and he knew she was embarrassed about cuddling up to him.

"Take your time," he called to her retreating back. "It's not as if we have appointments lined up this morning."

Five minutes later, he used another Sterno burner to warm water for instant coffee and cocoa. Emily wasn't a coffee drinker, but he was. Just one more difference.

When Emily entered the kitchen, there was still a heap of awkwardness between them. She was silent as they poured cereal. She was silent as she sliced a banana. She was silent as they sipped their beverages in Caleb Douglas's mugs.

Brad wasn't going to let her withdraw from him like this. If she was pregnant, they were going to have to keep communication open.

She was sitting at the kitchen table in a stream of sunlight that shone through the window. She'd tied her hair back in a short ponytail, and the style emphasized the perfect oval of her face.

"You said you have two sisters and a brother. What do they do?" he asked, choosing a safe topic.

"Eric is a history teacher."

"How much older is he than you are?"

"Two years. He got married right out of college and he and Sheila had kids right away."

"They still live in Chicago?"

"In Lyle." There was a fondness in her voice as she talked about her siblings. "Elaine's a paralegal. She's twenty-three, and Lizbeth will finish college this spring."

"Why didn't you start college after high school?"

Sadness passed over Emily's face. "I had other things to consider first." There was pride in her words as she explained, "Eric put himself through school and he'll be paying off loans for a long time. I knew if I went to college, I wouldn't be able to help Lizbeth and Elaine. So I went to a trade school for professional skills for a year and then entered the workforce. After Lizbeth finishes this spring, I'll be able to take the courses I told you about. It might take me a while, but I'll get my degree eventually."

Considering what she'd said, he realized she'd sacrificed her own education for that of her sisters' and sacrificed her own goals for her siblings'. He didn't know if he'd ever met anyone who had done that. His respect and admiration for Emily went up a few notches.

When she became silent again, he asked, "Are you worried about being pregnant?"

She didn't answer him but rose from her chair and took her mug to the counter. Then she poured more hot water into it and finally looked over at him.

"What's going through you mind, Emily? Tell me."

For a second she still hesitated, then finally answered. "I was in a serious relationship before I came to work at Vaughn Associates."

"How serious?" Brad asked, picturing her with another man and not liking the picture.

"Serious enough for me to be on birth

control. I wasn't careless about it, but I got pregnant."

That news hit him like a bucket of melted snow. "Do you have a child no one knows about?"

"No. When Warner found out I was pregnant, he wanted nothing to do with me or the baby. He was one of the partners in the law firm, and I was simply a secretary. I didn't realize until then he had been using me. I was just an afternoon treat, not a main dish… if you know what I mean."

Sometimes Emily's honesty made him uncomfortable. "And the child?"

"A few weeks after he broke it off and I quit my job, I had a miscarriage."

"Emily, I'm sorry!"

When he saw quick tears come to her eyes at his words, he went to her.

"It was a long time ago," she murmured. Her back was straight and she took an herbal tea bag from the box, opening it slowly.

"But apparently it's not forgotten."

Letting the tea bag dangle in the mug, she turned toward him. "I'll never forget. When I found out I was pregnant, it was a blow and it was going to complicate my life terribly, but I wanted that baby."

They'd had sex yesterday, and he'd held her in his arms last night. Nothing on earth could have kept him from hugging her now.

It pleased him when she laid her head on his shoulder as if it was a relief to lean on him. He had the feeling she didn't lean on many people—that she was the one who got leaned on.

Wanting to keep the situation between them honest, he growled, "I never should have put you in this position again."

"*I* was there yesterday, too," she said softly.

A low hum sounded through the cabin's walls and windows, becoming louder with each second.

Emily leaned away from him. "What's that?"

"It sounds like a helicopter. Maybe Caleb has sent the Marines."

When they grabbed coats and ran outside, they saw a helicopter had arrived. After it landed in the large clearing beside the cabin, they ran to it and met the pilot. He had indeed been sent by Caleb.

"We just have to put everything into our suitcases, then we'll be ready," Emily told him, her mood buoyant.

And that's about all it took.

She and Brad hurriedly folded the covers that they'd used and put them away, cleaned up the kitchen leaving supplies they'd bought and zipped up their suitcases. Minutes later they were in the rear of the helicopter and the pilot was lifting off.

Emily had been overjoyed when the helicopter had finally landed, but now, sitting beside Brad, staring out the window and leaving the cabin behind, she didn't feel quite so happy. Her days with Brad there had been…special. This morning when she'd told him about the miscarriage, he'd been so incredibly kind.

Now, could they go back to being boss-secretary?

When she turned her head, she could sense Brad was studying her. If only she could crawl inside his head and learn what he was thinking. On the other hand, maybe she didn't want to know.

If she'd been entertainment, if coupling had just been his way of passing the time, her heart was going to get broken.

The pilot had told them he was taking them to Caleb's ranch, the Lazy D, and as they flew to Thunder Canyon, Emily concentrated on her bird's-eye view of it so she didn't think about Brad and what had happened at the cabin.

Brad leaned close to her, and in a voice she could barely hear above the whirring of the propeller, he pointed below. "That's all Douglas land. There's the mine entrance."

She could see there were three access roads leading to one particular spot.

After the helicopter covered more distance, Brad motioned toward the mine entrance. "The erosion hole the boy fell into, where the rescue workers found the gold, was over one of the tunnels much closer to town."

The helicopter buzzed over Thunder Canyon Road, and she saw the Douglas ranch. There was a fantastically large two-story house, barns, fences and cattle grazing everywhere. Apparently Thunder Canyon had received a minimal amount of snow compared to the area where the cabin was located in the mountains. With the sun shining, all that was left of the snow here were sporadic patches.

After the pilot landed to the rear of the huge house, Brad took both suitcases, not hearing of Emily carrying hers. The look he gave her was dark and intense and she wondered again what was going to happen next. What did she *want* to happen next?

Caleb Douglas met them outside one of the back doors and waved them inside. But Emily was concerned with making muddy footprints on expensive-looking rugs, which she decided had to be Oriental. Inside they stood in a large room with a fireplace, pool table and an assortment of sofas and love seats. That one room was bigger than any apartment she'd ever lived in.

She slipped her shoes off and Caleb looked at her questioningly.

"I don't want to mess up your carpet or floor."

"The housekeeper will take care of that." He studied them both. "You don't look any worse for wear. I'm sorry you two got stranded up there for so long. I figured the power would go out with the snow and the wind. I want to get a generator up there but just haven't done it. I've been busy with the ski project. Anyway, I drove up there yesterday but couldn't get across the creek in my SUV. The helicopter wasn't available until today."

After a quick look at Emily, Brad answered, "We're fine."

Caleb went on. "The bad news is, no rooms

have opened up at the motel or the inn. The good news is, my wife's family left yesterday so you're welcome to stay here."

"We don't want to be in your way…." Brad began.

"This house is big enough. You won't be in my way. I also wanted to tell you I rented an SUV for you. Brought it in from Bozeman. You won't have any trouble getting around, no matter where you want to go, unless you want to cross the creek," he added with a wink.

A woman had slipped quietly into the room while they'd been talking, and now Caleb motioned her forward. "This is Tess Littlehawk, my housekeeper. She'll show you upstairs to your rooms."

Tess Littlehawk was a striking woman who looked to be in her forties. She had jet-black hair parted down the middle and bound in a thick braid. Her eyes were the darkest brown, almost black, and her broad face had lines around her eyes and around her mouth. She was wearing navy blue slacks and a matching tailored top with short sleeves that Emily guessed was a uniform of sorts.

"It's good to meet you, Tess," Emily said immediately.

"You too, miss," Tess responded.

"Take them up to their rooms now, Tess," Caleb ordered. "I'm sure they're going to want to get unpacked and enjoy some creature comforts after the past few days." He checked his watch. "After lunch, we'll meet in my den. I know you need an update on what's been happening here." Motioning toward the double doors that led out of the family room, he urged, "Go on now. If you need anything, just let Tess know."

When Brad reached for the suitcases, Caleb shook his head. "I'll have someone get those."

Brad picked them up anyway. "I'll take them up."

"Suit yourself." He saw Emily was carrying her laptop computer and a camera bag. "You might want to bring your computer along for our meeting—then you can type notes as we go. I'll expect weekly reports," he told Brad.

"That's what I intended," Brad assured him.

Minutes later they emerged from the family room onto more polished hardwood floors. Tess led them down a corridor, then into an immense foyer with a two-story-high ceiling. The sweeping staircase was also polished wood.

As she and Brad followed Tess upstairs, Emily saw mostly closed doors.

"This is the east wing," Tess told them. "Mr. and Mrs. Douglas are situated in the west wing. I haven't gotten all the rooms up here cleaned and swept yet, but these two are yours." She motioned to two open doors on the same side of the hall. "These rooms are connected by a bathroom. If that's not to your satisfaction, I'll have another cleaned in about an hour."

"It's up to you," Brad said, gazing down at Emily.

They'd just shared two days in a cabin with a single bathroom. "This is great," she murmured.

"Let me show you the setup." Tess led them inside.

The first bedroom was huge, with a king-size lodgepole headboard and a burgundy-and-hunter-green quilt on the bed. Vertical wooden blinds were open at the windows.

Tess kept going and opened a door that led into an opulent bathroom. There were two vanities, two sinks, a huge shower and a Roman tub.

Quickly Tess went to the second door on the other side of the bathroom and opened that. When Emily saw a lilac-and-yellow room, she knew no place would be more pleasant to sleep. It was absolutely beautiful, with its white spread with lilacs scattered all over it, Priscilla curtains and maple dresser, nightstand and headboard.

"This is wonderful," she told the housekeeper.

"Would you like me to unpack your suitcases for you?" Tess asked.

"I'll do mine myself," Brad said. "Emily?"

"I'll unpack, but I will need an iron and an ironing board."

"I'll take whatever you need ironed down to my suite and do it. I'm sure that's what Mr. Douglas would want."

Emily had no idea what it was like to be waited on. She accepted the offer. She didn't know how busy she and Brad were going to be after their conference with Caleb.

"If there's anything else you need," Tess advised them, "just use the intercom. Press the button for room three. If I don't answer there, dial in the number on the pad by the phone. Just call that and my pager will beep."

While Emily was trying to absorb that, the

housekeeper took another long look at Brad. "Mr. Douglas said that you were a private investigator."

"Yes, I am."

Emily thought the housekeeper was going to say more, but then she just gave them a tight smile and repeated, "Like I said, just buzz me if you need me. My rooms are behind the kitchen, so I'm always around."

Then she left Emily's room through the door into the hall.

"I'll get your suitcase for you." At the bathroom Brad stopped. "Are you sure this setup is fine with you?"

"Yes, it's fine with me."

"If you'd feel more comfortable about it, you can lock your door into the bathroom at night."

Then he went into the other bedroom, leaving Emily to wonder whether he was just being considerate of her feelings or if he was telling her they wouldn't be sleeping together again.

Chapter Five

Emily sat in Caleb Douglas's study in a tan leather chair, taking notes on her laptop. Every once in a while when there was a lull in Brad and Caleb's conversation, she admired the western sculptures sitting about—the cowhand on a horse, the cowboy on a bucking bronc—as well as the charcoal sketches of rodeo scenes hanging on the walls along with elk antlers.

After Brad's parting comment about keeping her door locked, he'd told her he'd go downstairs until she finished showering and then he'd take his. He'd wanted to get the lay of the land. Later, while she'd dressed, she'd heard him in the shower and remembered his musculature in the light of the fire.

She also remembered his strength and power as he'd made love to her.

"Emily, did you get that?"

Brought back to the present with a jolt, she realized Brad was speaking to her. "I'm sorry. Could you repeat what you said?"

He gave her an odd look. "The gold mine and the mineral rights to it were owned by Amos Douglas, Caleb's grandfather. He supposedly won the property in a card game."

"I thought the deed was in my safety-deposit box along with all the other deeds, but it wasn't," Caleb explained.

"Could another descendant of Amos Douglas have it?"

"I'm the last one. Riley has checked through all his papers, though he says he's never seen it."

"And you hired a lawyer to do a title search?"

"I hired an attorney in town. He found there's simply no record anywhere. I do have this, though." Caleb stood, went into the room adjoining the den, which Emily supposed was his study, and returned with an envelope. He handed it to Brad.

As Brad opened the envelope, Caleb warned, "Be careful. It's old."

Emily watched while Brad drew out a yellowed half sheet of paper.

"What is it?" she asked, more out of curiosity than for her notes.

"It looks like a promissory note. Someone owed Amos Douglas. Whoever it was agreed to pay Amos back twenty-five dollars a month. If the borrower missed a payment, the deed to this section of land…" He stopped and looked up at Caleb.

"That's the land where the gold mine's located," Caleb offered.

Brad continued, "The deed to this section of land plus the mineral rights would revert to Amos Douglas."

"Who signed it?" Emily asked.

"That's the problem." Brad ran his fingers along the edge of the paper. "I don't think this is torn, but it looks like the paper separated from the fold. It's over a hundred years old. No wonder." Brad looked up at Caleb again. "Do you think your great-grandfather foreclosed on this property?"

"It's not only possible, but likely. My father told me Amos was a shrewd businessman."

"Are there rumors about who this person was he foreclosed on? Where I'd have a place to start?"

"No rumors about the note."

"Searching the archives in town is probably the best place to start," Brad concluded. "Emily and I will head over there this afternoon."

"I also heard there's a reporter who's been asking questions," Caleb said.

"About the mine?"

Caleb looked discomfited. "This whole gold-rush thing has gotten bigger than anyone expected. A paper hired this reporter to do a story. I called him yesterday but he said he hasn't turned up the ownership. He wouldn't say much else. There was a baby crying in the background so it might have been a bad time. Maybe you can get more out of him."

"What's his name?"

"Mark Anderson."

"I'll call him today and set up an appointment." Brad stood and asked Emily, "Can you be ready to go over to the town hall in about ten minutes? I'd like to get there before it closes."

"Sure. Are you going to call Mr. Anderson?"

"Hopefully I'll catch him in."

Caleb handed Brad a scrap of paper. "There's his number. I hope you can figure out this whole mess. I know that land belongs to our family."

"I'll see what I can do."

Emily knew if anyone could get to the bottom of it, Brad could. When he was determined, he went after his goal, and heaven help anyone in his path.

From the street, Emily lifted her camera and snapped a photo of the town hall. As she and Brad walked up to the double doors, he said to her, "This could have waited until tomorrow if you're tired." She'd been very quiet since their meeting with Caleb.

"I'm fine."

He opened one of the doors for her. It was wood and heavy and it creaked.

Stepping over the threshold, she almost felt as if she was walking into the past. "This is one of Thunder Canyon's original buildings," Brad explained, then glanced at her because she didn't respond. "Are you thinking about our meeting with Caleb? Or are you thinking about our stay at the cabin?"

As they walked deeper into the reception area, they spotted a woman seated at a rough-hewn wooden desk.

"Both, I guess," Emily murmured, wishing he hadn't begun this conversation here. He must have felt the same because his look told her they'd finish later.

Crossing to the desk, he nodded toward the nameplate—Rhonda Culpepper.

"Are you Ms. Culpepper?"

"Sure am. Can I help you?" she asked in a chipper tone.

"I hope you can help us," Brad returned with a smile. "I'm looking for the archives room."

Rhonda's face took on a perplexed look. "Why ever would you want to go down there?"

"It's in the basement?" Emily asked.

"Sure is, and everything smells musty. It's much older than I am," she added with a little laugh, then went on, "but I'm afraid you can't go down there. The room's always locked. There are original documents, you understand. We can't have people just poking in them. Our last archivist was making sure all the information was put into computers."

"Your last archivist?"

"Yes, Saul Rindos. He went to college to be a historian, then couldn't find a job. So we hired him. But fortunately for him and unfortunately for us, a few weeks ago he found a position in a museum—on the East Coast, mind you."

"Who's in charge of the room now?" Emily asked.

"Well, nobody exactly. I guess Mayor Brookhurst, if it comes right down to it. He has the key. He won't let anyone in there until we have an archivist. We have a new one coming—Harvey Watson. He's due in about mid-June."

"I think the mayor will let us in," Brad said to Emily.

"Oh, no," Rhonda protested. "I'm afraid he won't. Not right now, anyway. First of all, he won't let anybody in that room without an archivist present, not even just to look. He's paranoid about it and the history of this town. But on top of all that, he's taking his vacation. Went somewhere in Wyoming to see a friend, I think. Anyway, he's got the key and won't be back until the middle of the month. He has to be back for Caleb Douglas's groundbreaking ceremony for his ski resort."

"When's that?" Emily asked.

"May twenty-third, I believe. We have quite a reception planned afterward. Maybe you two can come?"

"I'm hoping we'll be finished our work here by then," Brad remarked. "Did the mayor leave a number where he could be reached?"

"He and his friend are doing some traveling. From what I understand, he wants nothing to do with phones or contact from us until he returns. Said he gets hassled enough here. Doesn't want to contend with it on his vacation. You can't blame him."

"You said the archivist was entering information into the computer. Any idea if he did it in a particular order?"

"Well, that's another of our problems," she confided. "The archives have always been stored in the basement. Years ago, back in the late eighteen hundreds I think, there was a fire. We lost many of the ledgers. Just a while back, when we didn't have an archivist, we had flooding. Boxes were emptied, material was shifted around. So to answer your question, I doubt if anything is in much order. That's why we need another archivist to continue the work of the last one."

Moving his hand across his forehead, Brad said patiently, "Thank you for your help. Who might the mayor report to if he does call in?"

"He has a sister, Elma Rogers. Her number's in the phone book."

"Do you mind if I mention your name to her?"

"Of course not, go ahead. In fact, I'll give her a call tonight to tell her you'll be talking to her. That way she'll know you're not trying to sell her something."

With the reassurance that the mayor's sister was indeed a very nice lady, Rhonda bid them a good evening.

Outside, Brad and Emily looked at each other and smiled.

"She was helpful," Emily insisted.

"As far as it went. I could use some real help. I made an appointment with Mark Anderson for tomorrow afternoon. He said he and his wife have a new baby and she usually sleeps in the afternoons."

At the mention of the word *baby,* Emily's face clouded. It seemed there were so many land mines where they were concerned.

Instead of dwelling on that, Brad suggested, "Let's walk down to that western-wear shop. I want to buy you a coat so you won't freeze while we're here."

"I'm not going to let you buy me a coat."

If he said she should consider it part of her bonus, he had a feeling he'd be in trouble. If he said he wouldn't miss the money, he knew he'd be in just as much trouble. So he said, "I want you to charge it to my expense account. If you hadn't come to Montana, you wouldn't need it."

Her nose wrinkled as she thought about the logic in that. "What about you?" she asked.

He was wearing his denim jacket. "I brought a couple of flannel shirts, so I'll be fine. Emily, let me do this, all right?"

She took a terribly long time to answer but finally she agreed. "All right. But just something warm. Nothing elaborate."

"It's up to you to decide whatever you want." He knew what he wanted to do. He wanted to kiss that frown right off her face. He wanted to hold her again as he'd held her through the night. But he knew that might not happen, not ever again.

After they stopped at the car and locked

Emily's camera inside, they crossed to the western-wear store. The scent of leather was strong as they entered. But Emily didn't head toward the leather goods and jackets. Rather, she aimed for a rack that held the sign Women's Fleece.

Choosing a jacket from the rack, she tried it on. It was royal blue with black horses edging the zipper and armbands.

"You look pretty in that color," he said before he thought better of it.

Her gaze locked to his and she seemed to be asking him if he was giving her idle flattery.

After he stepped closer to her, he adjusted the stand-up collar on the jacket, his fingers brushing her hair. "I wouldn't have said it if I didn't mean it."

He couldn't keep from pushing a few strands away from her cheek. He couldn't help inhaling her sweet scent. He couldn't hold his libido in check anymore where she was concerned, and that annoyed him.

Backing away, he said offhandedly, "It's practical."

"Yes, it is. I'll be able to wear it in Chicago next winter." She looked at the tag on the sleeve. "And it's even on sale."

Her pleasure in that made him laugh. This was the first woman he'd ever taken shopping who considered a lower price to be better than a higher one.

Instead of taking Emily into his arms and giving her a hug and a kiss right then, he checked his watch. "We'd better be heading back if we want to get ready for dinner. Is there anything else you want to look at?"

Her gaze fell on a rack of western-style blouses. "I'll just be a minute." Moments later she was rifling through them. When she found a white one with a cowboy hat and lariat embroidered on one pocket, a horseshoe on the other, she smiled. "It will be a souvenir."

He knew better than to offer to pay for the blouse. Maybe he hadn't known Emily Stanton well in the six months she'd worked for him, but in the past few days he'd learned enough to fill an encyclopedia.

As soon as Emily met Adele Douglas later in the day, she was impressed.

"I'm so sorry I wasn't here this afternoon when you arrived," Adele said as she showed Emily and Brad into the dining room that night.

Adele had a warm and gracious manner. She wore her blond hair in a chin-length bob and had dressed for dinner in a green, long-sleeved sweater and wool slacks. Everything about her was sophisticated.

"We invited our son Riley to dinner to-night, even though he needs no invitation," she said with a sly smile, beaming at her son.

Riley looked to be around Brad's age, with black hair, green eyes and a killer smile. He was almost as handsome as Brad. Almost. Emily knew she was prejudiced.

After Riley shook her hand and Brad's, they all seated themselves around the large cherrywood table. The buffet along one wall held two highly polished silver candelabra. In the buffet's center stood a silver tureen. Tess Littlehawk was ladling soup out of it. Emily noticed the housekeeper eyeing Brad and she wondered why.

"When I want a good, home-cooked meal, I come over here and let Tess feed me," Riley joked.

"He eats here most of the time because of working on the ski resort with me *and* living only a half mile down the road."

"I'm surprised you didn't invite Justin, too," Riley commented blandly.

An odd look passed between Caleb and Adele. Finally Caleb explained, "I have another son, Justin...Justin Crane. Actually, I knew nothing about him until a few months ago."

Emily could see that Adele looked uncomfortable but she recovered quickly. "Justin just married recently," Adele added bravely, rallying from whatever thoughts she'd been having. "He married a dear girl we'd raised most of her life and always thought of as a daughter. I'm sure you'll meet Katie and Justin sometime soon, at the groundbreaking ceremony if not before."

"The groundbreaking for the ski resort?" Emily asked.

"Precisely," Caleb boomed. "We're having a fine party afterward in the town hall."

"I'm hoping we'll have this whole mine matter wrapped up before then," Brad responded.

"What did you find out this afternoon?" Caleb asked.

"Not much. We can't get into the archives until the mayor returns."

"Why not?"

"Apparently Mayor Brookhurst doesn't trust the key to the archives room to anyone. I'm hoping it's not necessary. I'm not going to sit around and wait until he gets back. Emily and I have an appointment with Mark Anderson tomorrow afternoon."

"I hear he has invested in the *Thunder Canyon Nugget,*" Adele offered.

"He has a good reputation as a writer," Riley commented. "Maybe he'll use those pages for something more than gossip."

Caleb laughed. "You young folk don't appreciate the power of knowing what's going on in the town."

Riley returned his father's smile. "I don't need to know whose horse ran away from his barn. Maybe Mark will concentrate on bigger issues."

"Such as the ski resort?" Caleb asked with upraised brows.

"I'm hoping we can pull in some high-caliber tourists," Riley admitted.

Adele, who was sitting around the corner of the table from Emily, leaned over to her. "If they start talking business, you and I are going to start talking fashion."

Everyone at the table laughed and the conversation turned to the food Tess was serving, which smelled absolutely delicious.

After dessert, Adele showed them to a sit-

ting room. Emily found herself in a striped
love seat with Brad very close beside her. For
the rest of the evening she had to concentrate
hard to keep her mind on the conversation.
He was wearing a tan, cable-knit sweater and
hunter-green corduroy slacks. He fit right in
here with Caleb and Adele and Riley. Emily
knew she didn't. Her hair wasn't styled in
the latest fashion. Her clothes weren't as fine
as Adele's. She kept her nails trimmed and
shaped, but they weren't manicured like her
hostess's. This wasn't the life she knew, and
she probably never would know.

Yet to Brad this was probably the norm.

When Tess asked if anyone wanted a
nightcap a while later, Emily couldn't help
but yawn. "I'm sorry," she said, embarrassed.

"You have no reason to be sorry," Adele
assured her. "You must have had a terrible
couple of days in that cabin with no power.
Now maybe Caleb will get a generator."

"And do something about that bridge," he
said decisively. "I'll have to get a civil engi-
neer in to look at it."

The evening broke up then. After Emily
and Brad bid the Douglases good-night, they
headed for the stairs.

As they walked up in silence, Emily felt

she had to say something. "Wouldn't you like to know the story behind Justin Crane?"

"How do you know there is one?"

"His name's different, and Adele looked uncomfortable when it was first brought up. My guess is there might have been an infidelity there."

"You'd make a good private investigator."

She glanced at him quickly to see if he was making fun of her.

"You would," he said seriously now as they reached the second floor. "You're intelligent, savvy and can read people well."

At her door they stopped. "I have trouble reading *you*," she admitted softly, hoping he'd tell her what was going on in his head...or, more importantly, in his heart.

"Ahh, Emily," he said with a sigh, running his thumb across her bottom lip, looking deep into her eyes. "You're a temptation. But I think we'll both be better off if we keep our minds on what we came here to do."

Was she a temptation he didn't want or need? So be it. "You're the boss," she retorted flippantly, as if the whole conversation hadn't mattered at all, as if his touch didn't burn and spark desire in every part of her body.

Opening her bedroom door, she forced a smile to her lips. "I'll see you in the morning."

Then she closed her door and leaned against it. She was going to lock all of her doors tonight, as well as her heart. Not to keep Brad out—but to keep herself from getting hurt.

As Brad drove to the new housing development on White Water Drive the following afternoon, he glanced at Emily taking in the scenery. She hadn't brought along her camera today. Yesterday when they'd walked down the raised sidewalk in Old Town, she'd snapped picture after picture.

"No photographs today?" he asked now.

"No, I'll keep my mind on what we're doing."

"Do you have more than one camera? Lots of photography buffs do."

"Oh, no. It took me a long while to save for that one."

"So that's why you handle it so carefully." He'd noticed how she held it, how she used it, how she carried it. He should have realized that if she was using her money to help her sister through school, she wouldn't have funds for more than one camera.

"What do you enjoy photographing the most?" he asked.

"People I love. Sometimes its hard getting candid shots of them. Scenery's a close second."

"What do you do with the pictures?"

"Some I frame for gifts, others that are good I donate to worthwhile causes—auctions and the like. I have two file boxes of them in my closet."

"Did you ever think of submitting them to magazines?"

"You haven't even seen them. How do you know if they're good enough?"

He shrugged. "I have a feeling anything you do meets a certain standard. You're that kind of lady."

Glad he didn't have to explain himself further, he pulled into the driveway of the ranch house on Wagon Wheel Drive. It was a white house, and as yet there were no trees planted anywhere—or grass, either, for that matter. It looked as if the residents might have just moved in.

After Brad parked in the drive, they exited the SUV and went up the walk. When Mark

Anderson opened the door, they heard a baby squalling.

"I'm Mark," he said, shaking their hands and motioning them inside. "Sorry about the noise," he called above the crying. "I thought Marissa would be asleep."

Inside the house, Brad noticed it was cozy. There was a stone fireplace and a mantel with family photos in silver frames. The living room furniture was casual and comfortable looking and it all seemed to be brand-new.

Mark Anderson appeared to be near forty. He was around six feet tall, lean and wore his dark hair long. His wife, Juliet, looked to be more around Emily's age. Petite, she had brown eyes and long dark hair. But she looked tired right now as she juggled her baby from her arm to her shoulder.

"Want me to take her?" Mark asked.

"No, I'll go back to the bedroom with her. You have a meeting."

The baby was waving her arms now and crying so hard that she was red faced.

Emily approached Juliet and her daughter. "Would you like me to try? I'm Emily Stanton, Brad's assistant, and I have two younger sisters."

"If there's anything you know how to do

to make her stop crying, go right ahead," Juliet said, a bit exasperated.

Fascinated, Brad watched as Emily took the infant from Juliet's arms. Holding the baby, she bent down to it, her hair hiding her face. She began making a sound into the baby's ear. It sounded like "Sssh, sssh, ssshoo." Over and over she did it until Marissa began quieting.

The little girl's parents looked on, amazed. As Emily shushed and rocked, the infant looked up at her. Mark asked, "What are you doing to her?"

Emily didn't answer, just continued making the noise and rocking for a few moments longer. Finally when Marissa was quiet, she smiled at the new parents.

"I heard about this pediatrician who made a video. Anyway, babies are comfortable in the womb. Coming out into the world is overwhelming. So when you make that noise in their ear and you rock them, they think they're back in the womb again."

"Why didn't they tell me that at the hospital?" Juliet asked, shaking her head.

"Maybe because they don't know or they've never tried it. I doubt if it's going to work every time, but it might work some of the time."

She bent down to the baby again and repeated the sound.

Little Marissa's eyes closed.

"Well, I'll be darned." Mark's face was a study in exasperation and appreciation.

"Would you mind taking her back to her nursery and laying her in her crib?" Juliet asked. "I'm afraid if you transfer her to me she'll wake up again."

"I don't mind at all." Emily checked with Brad. "Unless you need me?"

"No. Mark and I'll get started. Take your time."

As he watched Emily carry the baby down the hall with Juliet leading her, he knew she'd make a wonderful mother. She'd make a wonderful...wife? He didn't know where that thought had come from. A wife was the last thing he wanted. His mother's betrayal of his father had made him certain from an early age that marriage was a risky business. He'd been tempted to try it with Robin when he was too young and idealistic to know better, but she'd reinforced the idea that marriage wasn't in the cards for him.

"You have a beautiful daughter," he said to Mark, envying the man.

"I'm going to adopt her."

"I don't understand."

Mark motioned to the two easy chairs. Brad took off his jacket and settled in one.

Looking not at all embarrassed, Mark explained, "Juliet was seven months pregnant when I met her. I sort of ended up taking care of her, and after the baby was born, I figured out we belonged together. In fact, we just got married by a justice of the peace yesterday and we're planning a church wedding next month."

"You made that sound very easy."

Laughing, Mark shook his head. "Sure I did. Happily ever after *is* easy. It's getting there that's hard."

Getting there. A man had to want to get there to get there and had to believe there could be a happily ever after. Brad simply didn't.

That settled, he asked Mark, "So, what can you tell me about the Queen of Hearts gold mine?"

Chapter Six

As Emily stood at Marissa's crib looking down at her, her heart hurt for the baby she'd lost. Someday she wanted lots of kids...with the right man.

The little girl was sleeping now as Emily stepped away from the bed, glancing around the room. The walls were pale pink with a wallpaper border of dolls dressed in lavender, green and pink. The dresser and crib were a light wood, and there was a small, green, crocheted blanket hanging over the foot of the crib.

"This is handmade," she said in appreciation.

"My *abuelita* crocheted that. It's called a *covijita*. It's one of the few things I have left from my family. They're all gone now." She pointed to a bookcase that was rustic and scarred. "My father made that."

There was loss and grief in Juliet's voice but also joy in the sentimental value of the gifts her father and grandmother had given her. Emily liked this woman already.

Glancing at the baby again, Emily said with a sigh, "I'd like to stay here all afternoon and watch her, but I'd better go in there. I'm supposed to be taking notes."

"Mark said Mr. Vaughn is a private investigator. Is that what you do, too?"

She thought about what Brad had said, that she might make a good one. "No. Not yet, anyway. I'm his personal secretary and assistant."

"Mmm," Juliet said.

Emily felt as if she had to explain further. "He thought if I came along on this trip, it would go quicker and we could get back to Chicago sooner."

"You must have had quite an experience being stranded with Mr. Vaughn in Caleb Douglas's cabin."

Staring at Juliet wide-eyed, Emily asked, "How do you know about that?"

"Even though we've had an influx of tourists, Thunder Canyon is still a small town. Gossip travels fast. That helicopter created lots of questions."

Shaking her head, Emily was embarrassed. "So everyone knows Brad and I were in that cabin? Alone?"

At that Juliet grinned. "Yes, and they've made assumptions about that."

"Oh, terrific! Just what I always wanted— a tarnished reputation. Brad and I are boss and secretary and…"

"Friends?" Juliet filled in for her kindly.

Feeling a blush steal into her cheeks, Emily couldn't lie to Juliet. "I guess. Sometimes I'm not sure. We didn't even know each other well before those few days in the cabin, but we got to know each other better there."

"I see sparks between the two of you," Juliet said with certainty.

About to deny it, Emily decided not to. "There might be sparks, but that's it. We're very different."

"Mark and I were very different, too. But we're very happy now."

"A child is a wonderful bond."

"Yes, Marissa is a bond, and Mark thinks of her as his daughter. So do I, but she's not. We were just married civilly yesterday and we're having a church wedding in June."

"You're kidding."

"No. Our love is very new, but it's going to last forever."

Although Emily wanted to believe in that kind of love, the kind her mother and father had had, she didn't know if she could. It was true she was falling in love with Brad. She could admit that to herself now. She never could have made love with him otherwise. But she didn't know if it had anywhere to go.

"I'd really better see if he needs me."

When Emily reentered the living room, Mark and Brad were still talking about the tourists who had come into the area and all the business Caleb's ski resort would bring in.

"I hope it will generate tons of advertising for the newspaper," Mark admitted. "That's what a newspaper needs in order to be profitable."

As Emily sat on the sofa, Brad filled her in. "Mark can find no record of the Queen of Hearts property on the computer. If the title *is* recorded anywhere, it's in a ledger in the archives."

"I just didn't get around to digging further," Mark explained. "Marissa was born, then Juliet and I moved in here and got married. With buying into the paper, I haven't had time to pursue the story or worry about old records. I did find two other leads, though. And the truth is, I'd like an exclusive if anything comes of them."

"It's a deal. What have you got?"

"There's an old prospector who lives out on Thunder Canyon Road. His shack looks as if it will fall down if you blow on it. He couldn't tell me much, and I'm not sure his ramblings can be trusted, but he implied that a woman owned the deed to that mine."

"A woman?" Emily asked. "Wouldn't that be unusual back then?"

Mark shrugged. "I just can't imagine how it's true if Amos Douglas won the property in a card game."

"It might not have been that simple." Brad told Mark about the promissory note.

"Now that's interesting."

"You said there were two possible leads," Emily prompted.

"Yes, the other is a woman named Tildy

Matheson. Supposedly her grandmother was a friend of Catherine Douglas, Amos's wife."

"Besides your leads, I can also poke around at the historical society," Brad said.

"We might find out more about Amos Douglas there," Emily added.

"Is this Tildy reliable?" Brad asked Mark.

"Her memory's fading and she probably has stories handed down from her grandmother. But there's no way to know how they've changed in the retelling. Chasing down history is sometimes like trying to catch a wisp of smoke."

When Juliet came into the room, she was smiling. "Marissa's still sleeping."

"You might want to make a tape of shushing," Emily advised her. "Your voice and the sound could lull her to sleep when she's restless."

"You've got one smart assistant here," Juliet said to Brad, and Emily felt herself blush.

Whenever Brad focused his attention on her, it was as if she were the only person in the world—the only woman in the world. Now he did just that and she felt her whole body want to lean toward him, go to him, nestle in his arms.

"She's more than smart," he murmured.

His low voice led Emily to remember the husky sounds and erotic words they'd uttered to each other when they'd made love in his bedroll. From the sparks in his eyes, she wondered if he was thinking about that day, too.

"How would you two like to stay for dinner? Nothing fancy, just some carne asada and rice with a tossed salad."

Brad glanced at Emily, and she gave a little nod. She'd like to get to know this couple better.

"Sure, we can stay. I'll call Caleb and Adele so they don't expect us."

The talk before dinner and during it took many different roads. Mark had been everywhere and seen everything as he'd trotted the globe. His stories were engrossing. In the midst of the many topics of conversation, Emily pieced together that Juliet had come to Thunder Canyon alone. She'd only brought a few things and was waitressing at the Hitching Post, a local restaurant and saloon, when Mark had met her. Both of their lives had been changed drastically by that meeting. It was easy to see how happy they were. Mark was never far from his wife, encircling her with his arm, giving her a smile, touching her hand.

Later Emily and Juliet were loading dishes into the dishwasher when Marissa began crying again.

"This time she wants to be fed," Juliet explained. "I'll do that in the nursery, then bring her out so she can join us. She's usually a contented baby."

"Does Mark help you with her?"

"Oh, yes. In fact, he's insisting that I pump milk and try to give her a bottle some of the time so he can feed her, too. That way I can catch a few more hours of sleep and skip a feeding."

About fifteen minutes later, Emily and Brad were discussing visiting the prospector when Juliet brought Marissa into the room. Her terry playsuit, pink with little kitties printed all over it, was still too big for her.

Instead of settling in a chair or taking Marissa to Mark, Juliet went over to Brad and sat beside him on the sofa. Time after time, as they chatted, Brad looked down at the little girl with a tender gleam in his eyes.

Finally Juliet asked him, "Would you like to hold her?"

"I've never held a baby before." His voice was gruff, and Emily wondered what he was thinking about. Suzette's baby, maybe? The possibility he could be a dad?

"It's never too late for a man to get used to babies. Here, try it."

At first Brad was all thumbs, not knowing exactly how to hold Marissa. But with Juliet's gentle urging for him to support the baby's head, he took the little girl into his arms.

Emily wished she had her camera. The handsome man and the tiny baby would make quite a photograph. The expression on Brad's face was one she'd never seen there before. It told her that holding Marissa touched his heart in some way nothing else had ever done.

When he became comfortable with the infant, he ran his thumb across her chin and slipped one of his fingers into her tiny hand.

Marissa grabbed on to it reflexively and held tight.

Brad's gaze caught Emily's, and she felt herself in more turmoil at that moment than she had ever been in in her entire life.

Neither Brad nor Emily spoke much on their return trip to Caleb's. Emily knew the house would be empty except for the house-keeper. Caleb had told them he and Adele were going out after dinner.

Brad parked the SUV in the driveway. After he and Emily had gone inside and re-moved their coats, she wasn't sure what to do next. But Brad took her by the elbow and led her into the sitting room. "I'd like to talk to you about something."

She could feel his hand through the mate-rial of her blouse. The sexual buzz between them was exceedingly strong tonight.

After Brad guided her to the love seat, she sat there beside him, curious as to what he wanted to discuss. Caleb's case? A trip to the prospector? Mark and Juliet? The two of *them*?

"I've been thinking about something," he began. "I meant what I said—that you would be a good private investigator. When we get back, I think it would be a good idea for you to work with Jack McCormick."

Jack was a senior investigator, in his fifties and very good at what he did. "In addition to being your secretary?"

"No, in place of being my personal as-sistant and secretary. It would be a promo-tion, Emily. Your salary would go up and you could possibly get into the investigative work itself."

A tiny voice inside her head screamed, *I don't want to leave you,* but of course she wasn't going to tell *him* that. It was obvious he regretted what had happened between them in the cabin and now he was trying to find a way out of it.

"If that's what you think is best." Her voice came out stilted but she couldn't help that. She'd thought they were getting closer. She'd thought they were really learning to know each other. But she guessed Brad could see their differences now even more glaringly than he had before.

Wrapping her pride around herself, she added, "I know Mr. McCormick's well respected and he can teach me a lot."

"Is it what you want, Emily?"

She couldn't tell Brad what she wanted because it was a dream she could never attain. *He* was a dream she could never attain.

Maybe holding Marissa had made him realize he didn't want to deny being the father of Suzette Brouchard's baby. Maybe he'd realized fatherhood wouldn't be so bad. Maybe he was thinking about her becoming pregnant and how that would affect them working together. Even if she wasn't pregnant, nothing would ever be the same as it had been before this trip.

As if he'd read her thoughts, he assured her, "I haven't forgotten what happened between us in the cabin. If you are pregnant, I'll stand behind you and support you however I can. I don't want you to be afraid of that."

"I'm not afraid, Brad," she said quietly. "I've been managing my own life for a long time now. I'll manage no matter what happens."

Then, because she couldn't continue this conversation, because she couldn't look at him without wanting to kiss him, she stood to leave. "I'm going to go up to my room now and type up notes on what Mark told us. Afterward I'm going to turn in. I'll see you tomorrow."

Trying not to run away from Brad Vaughn, she walked slowly out of the room and up the stairs. Although her feelings for him were growing stronger, she realized that she was just going to have to get over them.

Brad raked his hand through his hair and leaned back against the sofa cushion. *That* hadn't gone well.

Emily usually voiced her opinion. If she'd wanted to continue to work with him, she would have said so, wouldn't she?

Ever since they'd arrived in Thunder Canyon, everything about Emily Stanton had gotten under his skin. It wasn't just her natural beauty that made him react to her. It was the essence of who she was—her down-to-earth nature, her compassion, her caring. When she'd held Marissa today and lulled her to sleep—

Brad had entertained visions of her carrying his child!

What if Emily was pregnant?

He didn't have an opportunity to answer the question as Tess came into the sitting room. "Mr. Vaughn, would you like something to eat or drink?"

"No, thank you, Tess. I might go out for a walk."

"Before you do, sir, can I speak to you?"

"Sure."

Tess came over to the sofa, looking anxious. "Since you're a private investigator, do you ever find missing persons?"

"Once in a while we'll take on a client like that. Why?"

After she seemed to debate with herself,

she answered, "I have a daughter who's missing. She was fifteen when she ran away. She'd be eighteen now. The year she left, I found this job with the Douglases, hoping to make more money so I could search for her. And I have. But traveling is so expensive and...I don't know where to go. But you...you probably have ways to find her. I have saved up some money and I wondered if you'd take on my case."

Without even asking how much money Tess had saved, Brad knew she could never pay what his agency expected. Somehow right now that didn't matter, but Caleb Douglas did. "I don't know how much the present case is going to tie me up in Thunder Canyon. Let me think about it and get back to you."

She looked happy he'd even consider taking her on. "I'd appreciate that. Are you sure you don't want something to eat or drink?"

"No, I'm going out for that walk."

Hopefully the Montana air would clear his head.

When Brad and Emily went looking for the prospector at his cabin on Saturday, to Brad's frustration, they couldn't find him.

The conversation the night before with Emily had caused a strain between them that was palpable, and they talked little. On Sunday morning, Brad had intended to try to reach Tildy Matheson instead of searching again for the prospector.

However, after breakfast Emily requested the keys to the SUV.

"Where are you going?" he asked.

"To church."

After he was silent for a few moments, he said, "I'll drive you."

Before they left he phoned the number Mark had given him for Tildy Matheson, but no one seemed to be home and he turned off his cell phone. No answer... They were batting zero.

Dressing for church, Brad realized it had been years since he'd attended a service. He found peace settling around him as he drove into town. The steeple of the pretty white church reached high into the blue sky as clouds puffed around it. The building was located on north Main Street and although it wasn't as old as the structures around the town hall, the cornerstone noted that it had been built in 1910.

After Brad parked in the lot behind the

church, townsfolk said their good mornings and strolled beside or in front of him and Emily, heading around to the front. Sun streamed through stained glass windows into the vestibule, creating rainbows on the tile floor. Two sets of double wooden doors led into the main body of the church. They were propped open, and Brad could see the pews were filling up fast. They walked up the middle aisle and found an empty spot at the end of the pew about ten rows back from the pulpit.

Brad had found his hand on the small of Emily's back as they'd walked up the aisle. An odd feeling of the rightness of being here with her confused him.

As they sat side by side in the pew, Emily leaned over and whispered to him, "Isn't this beautiful?"

He knew she meant the old wood and the stained glass windows and the interestingly carved pulpit that stood in the front. But all he could see was her face and the guilelessness in her beautiful green eyes.

"Yes, it is."

They were still gazing at each other when the organ music began. Startled, they reached for hymnals and opened to the hymn numbers posted on the board to the side of the front pews.

Discovering he remembered the old hymns, Brad's voice rose along with Emily's. Later he found himself listening intently to the minister's sermon about the bonds of family. He'd never known a close-knit family like the one the reverend spoke of. When he'd lived with his mother, he'd felt resentment that she'd broken her marriage apart. When he'd lived with his dad, he'd missed his mother and the softness of her presence in the big house. Over the years he and his father had become civilly polite to each other, but Phillip Vaughn had taken every opportunity to blame the collapse of the marriage on his wife.

Brad's mother had never talked to him about the divorce. She'd never defended herself. She'd never told him why she'd turned to another man. The odd thing was, she'd never remarried. After the affair that had torn their family apart, she hadn't even dated.

At the end of the service, the minister gave a blessing to the congregation, then made a few announcements. The second one made Brad's ears perk up.

"Matilda Matheson will turn eighty-five

this month. In honor of this milestone and all of the work she's done for this church over the years, we'll have a gathering in the church hall on May twenty-fifth. Everyone is welcome, and if you can't find time to join us, you can bid her a happy birthday after services today."

He pointed to one of the first pews on the right side of the church. "She's wearing a special birthday hat her niece gave her for the occasion, so you can't miss her."

Brad took note of a large blue felt hat decorated with feathers and flowers, then leaned close to Emily. "We'll have to stop and introduce ourselves. Maybe we can set up a meeting."

"Do you want to hang back until everyone's wished her a happy birthday?" Emily asked.

"That's probably a good idea."

Although the rest of the congregation filed from the pews a few minutes later, after their row filed into the aisle, Emily and Brad lowered themselves to the pew once more. The church emptied amazingly quickly. Chatter in the vestibule was loud as they sat in silence.

"The reverend's sermon made me miss my

family," Emily admitted in the hushed after-math of the service.

"Do you see them often?"

"I live with Mom. I can help Lizbeth better with college that way and I think my mother's glad for the company. Lizbeth doesn't get home every weekend. She finds rides with friends when she can, though she'll be home for the summer next week. My brother and his family and Elaine and her boyfriend usually join us for dinner on Sundays. How about you? I know you see your dad every day at work, but that's not the same as just keeping each other company."

"My dad and I have never just kept each other company," Brad responded in a wry tone. "After my parents' divorce, I spent weekends with him. My mother would drop me off Friday evening after school and he'd take me out to dinner somewhere. But then he usually worked the rest of the night while I watched TV. Saturdays he took me with him to the office. And Sundays we were just sort of there together until Mom came and got me in the afternoon. I'm not sure that was keep-ing each other company because we didn't talk. After I began college, I didn't see him much at all."

"Don't you spend any *fun* time with him now?"

"Fun? I'm not sure my father knows the meaning of that word. We go to so many business dinners that I guess it never occurs to us to see each other outside of that."

Emily's eyes were large and sparkling, her voice soft as she asked, "And what about your mother?"

"I've always thought my mother was as complicated as my father. I went to school, did my homework and she'd have the requisite cookies and milk ready while I was doing it. She can talk about anything under the sun and fill up any silence. But I don't think we've ever had a serious conversation, not about anything that really matters."

"Like what?" Emily prodded.

"Like life and its pitfalls and rewards."

"Do you bring girls home to her when you're dating?"

That must have been some standard to Emily, so he answered honestly, "I did once. I met someone when I was in college and I brought her home with me for the weekend."

"Did your mother like her?"

"Actually, she didn't. Back then I thought she was against Robin for the same reason my father was. She came from a different side of life than I did. Her dad was the foreman in a clothing factory and her mother waited tables. My mother hadn't smiled much that weekend. She'd been polite to Robin but not completely welcoming."

"You said 'back then.' Do you see another reason now?"

"Maybe my mom saw a flaw in Robin that I didn't."

"I don't understand."

Until now Brad had never told anyone what had happened. Today, though, looking into Emily's honest face, he revealed, "My dad offered her money to stop seeing me. She took it and flew to the West Coast."

"Oh, Brad."

He shrugged. "I got over it. After all, I guess my father did me a favor if that's all Robin cared about."

"Your father should have let you discover it on your own."

Because Emily said that with such certainty, Brad asked her, "You advocate the school of hard knocks?"

"I'm not saying experience is the best teacher, but it's a good teacher. We learn from our mistakes."

"Oh, I learned from my mistakes. After that I didn't date girls from the wrong side of the tracks."

When he saw Emily's expression, he immediately realized what he'd said and how she'd taken it. "Emily, I didn't mean anything by that. That reference had nothing to do with you."

"My father was a blue-collar worker, too, but I don't think degrees of wealth have anything to do with integrity and moral fiber. I understand that you didn't want to risk the same thing happening again so it was easier to date women from the same circles you were in."

"Maybe I'm learning that was a mistake. Suzette had money of her own and now she's asking for more. I should have realized sooner how to find a woman with integrity."

He wanted to tell Emily that *she* was a woman of integrity, but after the remark he'd made, she'd think he was just trying to mend fences. He knew exactly what she was thinking—he'd slept with her but he didn't want to date her.

"The crowd is thinning back there," she said quickly in a soft voice.

Longing to put his arm around her, he

wanted to draw her close and kiss her forehead and tell her she was the sweetest woman he'd ever met, though the most frustrating, too, sometimes. But he didn't have that freedom. Until this matter was settled with Suzette, Emily would believe he was an irresponsible playboy. Maybe he *had* been a playboy once, but this trip was changing his view of the world. And maybe it would change him, too.

After they walked to the vestibule, they waited until Tildy was finally alone.

Approaching her, Emily said, "Happy birthday, Miss Matheson."

Tildy's gray hair was straight and cut at her wrinkled double chin. She was stocky with substance to her and leaned on a cane. Her blue eyes twinkled as she asked, "Do I know you, child?"

"No, you don't. My name's Emily Stanton and this is Brad Vaughn. Mark Anderson spoke about you to us, and we wanted to say hello."

"Well, how kind of you. So many people have wished me well today. If all their wishes would just take away my arthritis, I'd be the happiest old-timer in town. I can't even do those front steps out there. I'll have to go out the side. But I guess that's a small price to pay for reaching eighty-five."

Brad stepped in then. "Actually, I tried to phone you this morning."

"You did? My niece picked me up to take me to breakfast before the service. In fact, I'm going home with her afterward. She's driving me to Billings so I can spend time with my sister."

Frustrated, Brad felt as if they were being stalled on all fronts. "The reason Mark mentioned you to us, the reason I called, is because we wanted to talk to you about whatever you know concerning the Queen of Hearts gold mine."

Just then a woman who might be close to sixty came up to Matilda Matheson. "Aunt Tildy, we should go."

Tildy introduced her niece Amelia to them. Then, returning to their earlier conversation, she told Amelia, "They want to come by and chat. I imagine I'll need to rest some when I get back on May twentieth. I don't travel as well as I used to. How about the day after that? You could come for tea."

Although Brad had wanted to get this trip over with as soon as possible, the fates were conspiring against him. Maybe he should stop pushing and go with the flow. Maybe he'd find the deed before Tildy returned and he wouldn't need to meet with her. However, keeping his options open, he said, "That will be fine. We'll call you when you get back and set up a time."

Emily smiled at Tildy. "You have a wonderful trip, Miss Matheson."

"Call me Tildy."

"We'll do that," Emily assured her.

As her niece took her arm and they walked back into the church to go out the side entrance, Emily asked, "We're going to be here until May twentieth?"

The twentieth was twelve days away. "I hope not. But it depends on how much progress we make. If you want to fly back to Chicago, I understand."

"No," Emily said quickly. "I mean, I said I'd help you with this and I will. Besides, Thunder Canyon is growing on me."

He had to smile…because it was growing on him, too. And so was Emily Stanton.

Chapter Seven

"I've never ridden a horse!"

As Emily stood looking up at the mount Caleb's foreman had brought into the corral for her, she felt total dismay. "Do *you* go riding?" she asked Brad, who was standing beside her.

"Not much anymore. I spent that summer in Montana years ago with a college friend. And I ride on vacations."

She fingered the camera strap on her shoulder. "I don't know if I should do this. What if I'm—"

"Pregnant?" Brad filled in, moving closer to her.

She nodded.

"You don't have to go riding. Don't do it just to impress Caleb. But if you want a taste of the experience, I'll help you into the saddle, and we can just walk our horses."

Thinking about it, she rolled the idea over in her mind. She'd heard that sitting on a walking horse felt the same as being in a rocking chair. Probably she'd never have the chance for this experience again. "Walking should be safe enough."

She glanced at the mount Caleb had chosen for her, a very old bay gelding named Calypso. "I'd like to try it. Maybe I can take more film of this beautiful scenery."

The foreman motioned to her to come closer to the barn. He'd left a hay bale there and was holding the horse beside it.

Brad's hand was on her shoulder as they approached Calypso, and she liked the feel of it there. Brad was so different here than in Chicago. Here he was a real person, not a rich man in a suit who could get whatever he wanted.

After she handed her camera to the foreman, she stepped up onto the hay bale. With care, Brad showed her how to put her foot in the stirrup and how to swing her leg over.

In a matter of seconds, she was sitting in the saddle, feeling as if she were on top of the world. The horse lifted his head and then lowered it again.

Brad advised her, "Take the reins and get a feel for them. If you pull back, he'll stop. If you loosen them, he'll put his head down or go."

"Pressure on his flanks with your feet will also help push him forward," the foreman explained. "You'll get the hang of it."

Clearing her throat, she said to Brad again, "I just want to go slow. Nothing fast."

His gaze met hers and she saw that he understood.

When the foreman handed her her camera, she slipped the strap over her head.

As she did that, she noticed Brad running his hand up and down her horse's nose, scratching between his ears. He was comfortable with the animal. Too well she could remember him touching her. Her cheeks heated up and she took the reins in both hands.

A few minutes later, when Brad climbed into his saddle, Emily realized he more than remembered how to ride a horse. He looked as if he belonged on one.

After Caleb and Adele joined them in the

corral, they mounted their horses. Adele rode a gray that was about the size of Emily's horse, while Caleb and Brad's steeds were larger and chestnut brown.

The walking motion of the horse was soothing. Emily felt more confident as the clip-clop of Calypso's hooves mingled with the lowing of nearby cattle and the chirping of birds. For a while they rode along the trail that followed the fence line. The scenery *was* awesome. Some of the ground was still snow-covered in shaded patches, and the firs were high against the immense blue canopy of sky. Breathtaking mountains stood in the distance, and Emily considered the fact that she certainly couldn't see scenery like this in Chicago.

When she glanced at Brad riding next to her, she felt a thrill just being here with him. She was actually glad they couldn't talk to Tildy until she returned. Emily wanted more time here with Brad.

When she heard the growl of an engine somewhere in the distance, she automatically gripped her reins tighter.

"You said you were in Montana years ago?" she asked Brad.

"On a ranch north of Billings.

"You seem to like it here a lot. Why didn't you ever come back?"

When Brad didn't answer, she glanced over at him.

The wind tossed his horse's mane, and he looked very somber when he finally responded, "I came out here that summer with a friend, James Lawson. We were roommates in college. I had to make some money, and jobs in Chicago were scarce and boring. I saw an ad in a magazine. The ranch needed hands and the pay wasn't too bad. It included room and board, so anything we made was pure profit. I think that summer was one of the most enjoyable of my life."

"Then why haven't you returned?" she asked again.

"When James and I were seniors, he found out he had leukemia. A year and a half later he was gone. I don't think I ever wanted to come back here without him."

Now she understood Brad's reluctance to return to a beautiful place where he'd only remember loss. His life hadn't been a joyride, either, and maybe that's why he kept emotional barricades in place. She felt as if she was really getting to know him now. "I'm sorry you lost him."

When Brad didn't respond, Emily understood that his loss hadn't diminished with time.

Up ahead Caleb and Adele crossed an access road. "I'm holding you back," she said to Brad. "If you want to ride ahead…"

"No. This pace is fine. I'm learning all over again how it feels to relax. This has got to be the best way to do it. If you want to snap photos, I'll hold your horse."

Drawing up beside her, he took her reins while she lifted her camera from around her neck and took one shot after another. Suddenly she turned toward *him* and began snapping.

"What are you doing?"

"You're part of the scenery."

He shook his head. "That's enough, then, if you can't find anything better than me." When he handed her back her reins, their hands brushed and she gazed up into his eyes.

He said simply, "I'm glad you're here with me, Emily."

Not knowing how to react to that, she started her horse walking again, reins in one hand, her camera in the other.

The rumbling of a car grew louder and

Brad frowned. "Whoever that is, they're going much too fast—"

The topless blue Jeep raced into view, speeding along on the gravel access road. It was occupied by four men wearing large hats. Immediately Emily stopped her horse. But before she knew what had happened, the Jeep backfired once, then again. Her mount reared up and took off at a run. When her camera fell to the ground, she hung on to the reins, scared out of her wits. Instinctively she wrapped the reins around one hand, trying to hang on yet pull back at the same time to make Calypso stop.

Nothing worked.

As she joggled in the saddle, suddenly Brad was racing beside her. He couldn't seem to catch Calypso's halter, so instead...

She felt more than saw him as he leaned closer to her and wrapped his arm around her. But as he pulled her away from her horse, her hand was still wound up in her reins and she felt her wrist wrench sideways.

Pain shot up her arm.

While Brad held on to her, she frantically wiggled her fingers. Finally the reins loosened, fell away, and Calypso raced ahead of them.

Practically in Brad's lap now, she held her breath until his horse stopped. Then he let her slide gently to the ground. Her legs were shaking so badly, she sank down onto the damp earth, trying to gulp in air as she heard the fading sound of Calypso's hooves.

Then Brad was beside her, his arm around her.

"Take it easy," he suggested. "Get a few breaths."

Finally her lungs seemed to work as she sucked in air and then sucked in more of it.

Bending over her, Brad's face was close to hers. The huskiness in his voice told her he was worried about her.

"I'm fine," she murmured, but as she braced her hand on the ground to scramble to her feet, she yelped. Her wrist hurt.

Brad rose quickly. "What is it?"

She knew she couldn't hide the injury from him. "My wrist."

"I'm driving you to the emergency room." Gently he took her hand in his. "Move your fingers," he ordered. When she did, he looked relieved. "I don't think it's broken. But I want you checked out."

"How am I going to get back?"

"With me." He'd tethered the reins to his

horse around some brush. "Come on, I'll help you into the saddle. Believe me, I won't let anything else happen to you."

She believed him. "My camera…"

"I know where it fell." He lifted her onto the saddle and she swung her leg over the pommel. "I'll walk you over there before I climb on."

Five minutes later, he'd found the camera, handed it to her and swung up onto the horse behind her. His arms were around her as he held the reins.

With his lips close to her ear, his breath was warm on her neck as he asked, "Ready?"

She almost felt ready for anything with Brad. She knew she was beginning to rely on him, and that scared her most of all.

Thunder Canyon General Hospital was a relatively new two-story building, surrounded by a parking lot. Brad bypassed the main entrance and headed for the E.R., pulling in as close as he could to the emergency-room door. A few minutes later, he guided Emily under the covered portico.

She stopped and took hold of his arm. "I'll have to tell the doctor I might be pregnant. If you don't want to be around, I'll understand."

"I'm not going anywhere," he responded gruffly.

The emergency room had pale blue walls and a white tile floor. The waiting room was pleasant in blue, green and lilac, with tall windows that allowed the late afternoon sun to stream through.

After Emily registered, she sat and waited until her name was called. Then she was taken down a hall into a room with several beds where blue-and-white-striped curtains hung between each.

"Dr. Taylor will be in shortly," the nurse informed them with a smile.

"I'd better give this to you," Emily said to Brad as she realized she still had her camera around her neck. When she lifted it off, she looked at it and a gasp escaped her.

"What's wrong?"

"I think the lens is cracked. It is. Oh, Brad…"

Her voice broke and Brad realized this whole incident had caused more trauma than she wanted to admit. He also knew how much that camera meant to her.

"Let me see."

When she handed it over, he noticed the tears in her eyes, and instead of looking at the camera he put his arms around her and brought her close.

"It's okay. Maybe I can get it repaired."

"I doubt it."

He guessed how long she'd saved to buy that camera. He knew her pictures probably expressed a part of her that she was afraid to express on her own.

Putting his hands on either side of her face, he tipped her chin up to him. "I'm just grateful you're okay. If you *are* pregnant, I don't want anything to happen to our baby."

She gave him a little smile now. "I know."

"You're an amazing woman," he whispered, his lips hovering tantalizingly just above hers.

Temptation was so great, he couldn't resist. When he kissed her, it was as if he were coming home. They hadn't kissed since their stay in the cabin. They hadn't touched deliberately since they'd made love. He missed her kisses and her touching as if he'd been used to it for a whole lifetime. As his tongue danced with hers and she responded to it, he thought about their separate bedrooms with the bathroom in between. He thought about asking her into his bed again tonight. He thought about—

Someone cleared his throat.

When Brad broke away, there was a tall man with wavy blond hair and blue eyes standing in the cubicle. He was wearing a lab coat and a stethoscope and Brad supposed he was the E.R. doctor.

"I'm not sure that's the medicine I'd prescribe for a twisted wrist." His eyes were filled with amusement.

Brad instantly went on alert because the doctor was good-looking, but then he noticed the gold band on his hand and felt relieved. When had he developed a possessive streak?

Not giving an explanation for their kiss or why he was in the cubicle with Emily, Brad stated, "It's possible she might be pregnant."

His smile fading now, the physician extended his hand to Emily and then to Brad. "I'm Dr. Taylor. I'll examine your wrist, then if you want I'll page an obstetrician."

Emily nodded.

After the doctor took a hospital gown from a cupboard and handed it to her, he glanced at Brad. "When we're finished, I'll send someone to get you in the waiting room."

Brad wanted to stay but knew he had no right to. With a last look at Emily, with her camera in his hands, he left the cubicle and went to sit in the reception area, worrying about her in a way he'd never worried about a woman before.

An hour later a technician came to fetch Brad and take him back to Emily. She was dressed again, and the doctor had just finished wrapping her wrist.

Emily explained to Brad, "It's too soon to know for sure if I'm pregnant. The obstetrician told me I can have a blood test in a few days or use an early-testing pregnancy kit in a day or two."

Dr. Taylor focused on Brad now. "She seems fine except for her wrist. She preferred I not X-ray it, and that's wise under the circumstances. But I think it's just sprained. If it's not better in a few days, come back and we'll decide what to do. She told me what happened…about the prospectors in the Jeep." The young physician looked almost angry.

Crossing the room, Brad stood by Emily. "I guess that can be expected when there's a rumor of gold."

"People coming here for Caleb Douglas's resort are one thing. They're investing in the area and they're going to have a stake in our lives, too. But the fly-by-nighters who are just looking for an easy buck or a few nuggets of gold don't care what they do to our town."

"They help the economy, though," Brad pointed out.

"Yes, they do, and the sudden influx of revenue for everyone will help make improvements in the hospital. I guess we can't stop any of it now. I heard the gold mine even made CNN."

Brad felt as if he and Emily had been isolated from the real world for weeks—and it had only been six days. "Thunder Canyon might grow faster than anyone wants it to."

"That's what I'm afraid of," the doctor agreed. Then he smiled. "But in the meantime, I'll just do what I do."

Turning to Emily, he added, "Being rescued from a runaway horse isn't an everyday occurrence. It wouldn't hurt to take it easy tomorrow. Keep ice on the wrist for the next twenty-four hours. A warm bath tonight might help relax you. If you have any unusual symptoms—dizziness, nausea, cramping—you come back in here. You hear?"

Although Emily nodded, Brad said, "I'll make sure she does."

At that, her gaze caught his and held.

Breaking eye contact, he walked her into the reception area and led her to a chair. "You stay here while I buy ice packs at the pharmacy."

"You don't have to do this—" Her voice caught.

"I know I don't. I also know you'd do the same for me."

With a smile that seemed to knock the wind out of her sails, he watched her as she sank down into a chair and picked up a magazine. She might be the epitome of the independent woman, but he'd found a much softer side to Emily Stanton, too. And he liked it.

When Emily and Brad returned to the Lazy D, Adele and Caleb were both solicitous and wanted to know what they could do to make her feel better. She simply smiled, gave them her "I'll be fine" speech and then said she was going up to her room to rest.

"Dinner will be ready in fifteen minutes," Adele advised her.

"I think I'll skip dinner tonight."

After she mounted the stairs, she made it to her room and lowered herself onto the bed.

Brad followed her. "I put the ice packs in

the freezer. The doctor's orders said fifteen minutes every hour. He said a warm bath might help relax you, too."

"I just want to go to bed."

"Not going to listen to doctor's orders?"

She wrinkled her nose at him. "Don't parent me, Brad."

"Believe me, the last thing I want to do is parent you."

When she saw the glimmer of desire in his eyes, she remembered how he'd kissed her so tenderly yet with so much passion at the emergency room. Dealing with that on top of everything else was just a little bit too much.

"Just leave me alone, okay?"

Coming over to her, he hunkered down in front of her. "No, I'm not going to leave you alone. I'm going to draw you a warm bath. When you're finished, I'll put ice cubes in a plastic bag for your wrist until the ice packs are ready. So get undressed, put on a robe and come into the bathroom in about ten minutes. If you don't appear, I'll come and get you."

"You can be so arrogant," she mumbled under her breath.

Even though it had been low, he'd still heard it. Rather than being offended, he grinned. "I know I can. It's a great way to get my own way. Ten minutes, Emily."

After he disappeared into the bathroom, she heard water running in the tub.

She didn't know whether to laugh or cry. Whoever could have imagined Brad Vaughn would draw her a bath. That was as crazy as this whole trip had been. But she did know Brad always got what he wanted and she didn't have the energy to fight him, so she did as he suggested.

He was still in the bathroom, standing over the tub, when she finally went in, her robe belted tight. Bubbles floated everywhere and the sweet scent of lavender hovered in the air.

"It's ready." He looked her over, making no move to leave.

"If you think you're going to stand here and watch me take a bath, you're sadly mistaken," she teased.

With a chuckle, he shook his head. "Somehow I knew you'd say that. I'll leave. But I won't be far away. Just yell if you need anything."

When he'd shut the door to his room partway, she laid her robe over a small settee and stepped down into the water. It did feel heavenly. Sinking beneath the bubbles, she let her head loll back, resting her bandaged wrist on the side of the tub.

For the most part Emily kept her eyes closed while she soaked, but every once in a while she'd hear Brad moving about in his bedroom. There was something totally intimate about having him close by.

Ten minutes later the water began to grow tepid. Shivering, she stepped out of the tub, dried off and belted her robe. Then she went to the door to Brad's room. "I'm going to bed now."

"Don't lock your door. I'll bring up the ice."

As Brad went downstairs, he thought about Emily's bath and how he'd wanted to join her in the tub. Then he remembered her body naked in the cabin shadows. It was an image he couldn't get out of his head.

When he entered the kitchen, he noticed Tess was putting the last touches on supper.

"How's Miss Emily?" she asked.

"Stubborn."

The housekeeper smiled, and then silence permeated the kitchen. Brad knew why. Tess wanted to know if he'd thought about taking her case.

In the midst of everything else, he had.

He was stalled here in Thunder Canyon at least for a while. He might as well do something worthwhile with his time. Truth be told, Tess's case was the type of challenge he'd like to take on. "I've given some thought to finding your daughter."

"You'll do it?" Her face looked brighter than he'd seen it since he'd arrived.

"I don't want to give you false hope, Tess. I might come up with zero. It's been a long time and some people who don't want to be found manage ways to keep hidden."

"She left because she was rebelling. She wanted to find her own way and I wouldn't let her. But maybe now she's just too ashamed to come home."

He knew that often happened. "That still doesn't mean I can find her, but I'll try. I want you to write down absolutely everything you know about her—where she liked to go, what she liked to do, who she liked to be with. I want a list of names—any friends who are still around, anybody she talked to. I also want a list of stores where she used to buy her clothes, purses and shoes."

Tess looked puzzled. "Why?"

"Although she may have wanted to run away from her life, people have habits and certain preferences. If we do come up with a location or vicinity and we don't have an address, I never know what might help. So just do it, okay? Write a book if you have to. Even the smallest details are important."

"I'll do it tonight."

Feeling good about taking her case, not knowing where it was going to lead, he asked, "Can I have a tray for Emily?"

"Sure. What would you like? I can warm up something."

"I don't think she's going to go for a whole lot. Maybe a sandwich and a glass of milk?"

"Just give me a couple of minutes."

Ten minutes later, Brad was carrying a tray up to Emily's room along with a plastic bag of ice wrapped in a towel. For courtesy's sake, he rapped on the door.

"Come in."

She was propped up on three pillows examining her camera. "I hope somebody can fix it."

"After we get back to Chicago, I'll find someone who can. In the meantime, you might want to buy one of those disposable cameras."

"That's a good idea. I hate to miss shooting anything I might want to remember."

Their eyes caught and held. She'd snapped a few pictures of him. Maybe she didn't have as many regrets as he thought she'd have over what had happened in the cabin.

When he took the tray to the bed, he could smell lavender. Her skin was a pretty pink from her bath. She was wearing a pink flannel nightgown, and all he wanted to do was crawl into bed beside her and hold her through the night as he had the last night in the cabin.

Setting the tray on her lap, he advised her, "You'll feel better if you eat something."

"I know." She said it with so much resignation he had to smile.

"Just put your tray outside the door when you're finished. Tess said she'll pick it up."

Emily took a few sips of the milk and nodded.

At the door, he turned to her again. "I told Tess I'd take on her case." He'd confided in Emily that Tess wanted him to search for her daughter.

"Do you think you can find her?"

"I don't know. She's supposed to write up some information tonight. I'll see where that leads. In the meantime, I'm going to search for the prospector again."

"I want to go along."

"It would probably do you good to sleep late. But I'll check with you before I leave."

He hesitated only a fraction of a second before he suggested, "I want you to keep your door to the bathroom open tonight. I'll do the same with mine. If you need anything, then you can call me."

To his surprise, she didn't argue or protest. Instead she just murmured, "Thank you, Brad."

Before he kissed her and decided to crawl into bed beside her after all, he went out into the hall and closed her bedroom door behind him.

Chapter Eight

Late Sunday evening, Brad's cell phone rang and he wondered if the caller was his father. He'd talked to him when they'd returned from the cabin and also checked in with other investigators who were working on projects under Brad's direction. They all had his cell phone number.

"Vaughn here."

"Brad, it's Mark Anderson. Did you find the prospector?"

"Not yet. I'm going out searching again tomorrow. If he went off for the weekend, maybe he'll be back."

"Besides his hut, I also heard about a spot where he camps out."

"Can you give me directions?"

"Do you want company? It's rough trekking. We'll have to hike about a mile to where I'm thinking about."

Brad explained about Emily's runaway horse. "I'll pick you up around nine. If Emily's still sleeping, I won't wake her."

"Nine sounds good."

The following morning, Brad checked on Emily. She was curled on her side, breathing evenly, her one hand tucked under her cheek. She was all feminine and pretty and soft and he wanted to hold her again.

Just hold her?

There was no way he was going to wake her simply to tell her where he was going. Finding paper and pen in his room, he wrote a brief note and laid it on the bathroom sink where she'd be sure to see it.

Twenty minutes later, he'd picked up Mark and they were headed out of town.

"So what's this guy's name?" Brad asked.

"Miles Latimer. But everyone calls him Mickey."

"What does he do out here?"

"He digs in the ground for gold, pans the streams. He has a favorite spot. He told me where it is, but I forgot to mention it to you."

"He digs for gold with a shovel?"

"A pickax and a spade."

"Who's property is he on?"

"I think it's part of the disputed Douglas property, but no one keeps him from doing it. He's causing no harm. It's rugged land and thickly forested."

"You make it sound as if I should have brought my survival gear," Brad joked.

"You never know."

Fifteen minutes later, Mark directed Brad to take a gravel lane. "It's an old logging road," he said.

The SUV rumbled and jumped over dips and ruts and potholes until finally they came to a stop and could go no farther. "We walk from here," Mark explained.

After they hiked through pines, up inclines and over a flat area for about a mile, Mark pointed to smoke billowing toward the sky. "There he is. He has a fire going this morning."

"It got pretty cold last night. He stays out in the weather?"

"Weather doesn't seem to bother him."

"How old is he?"

"My guess is around seventy, maybe seventy-five. He looks about a hundred and twenty, though. Yo, Mickey," Mark called, announcing his presence. "I don't want to sneak up on him. If he's paranoid, I won't appreciate looking down the barrel of a shot-gun."

In the clearing, a blue tent was a bright color of contrast against the landscape. A campfire was going about ten feet from it, and a man was hunched down at it.

"Do you mind if we talk to you?" Mark asked as he came closer to the man.

Brad could see that Mickey Latimer might have been a tall man at one time, but now he was stooped as he gazed into the fire. Dressed in jeans and a down parka that had seen better days, he also wore a leather hat pulled down over his eyes. The wide brim shaded his face and almost hid it. Ignoring Mark, Mickey poured coffee from a tin pan into a foam cup.

"Sometimes I think he's hard of hearing. Other times I believe the gossip and think he's just senile," Mark explained to Brad.

Approaching Mickey, he hunkered down

beside him. "I brought someone along who wants to talk to you, too. Do you mind?"

The old prospector gave Mark a look from under the brim of his hat. "Don't mind nothin'. I'm too old to mind anything."

Brad crouched down on the other side of the man. "Nice tent you have there."

The old man's eyes narrowed. "Don't you think about stealing it." As quick as lightning, he brought a pistol out that had been tucked in his back waistband.

"I wouldn't think of it," Brad assured him, giving Mark a look that asked if he really was dangerous. To make sure Mickey knew he was no threat, he sat on the ground beside him. "I'm not interested in your tent. I'm interested in what you know."

Mickey's focus went to Mark again. "What's he talking about?"

"Remember I asked you questions about the Queen of Hearts mine?" Mark asked.

"The mine. I have a mine."

Brad played along. "Where's your mine?"

Mickey motioned behind the tent. "Back there. Staked it out and everything. Do you want to dig with me?" There was a conspiratorial air about him.

"Maybe another time," Brad answered seriously. "I came to Thunder Canyon to find out if the Douglases really own the Queen of Hearts."

The prospector put a finger to his lips. "Shh."

Brad cast a look around him, then he caught on. "You know a secret?"

With a shrug, Mickey answered, "Maybe I do, maybe I don't. Maybe I remember things, maybe I don't."

"How old are you?" Brad asked.

The elderly man's face screwed up and he pushed back the brim of his hat. Brad could see his weathered countenance clearly now. It was long and lean and his eyes were blue and cloudy. His leather gloves were scraped and torn, and now he put a finger to his chin. "I don't rightly know. I can't remember. Maybe I have a birthday today."

Beginning to think they wouldn't get anywhere, Brad agreed, "Maybe you do."

"Don't want no birthday cake, though. It will rot my teeth. Did you come to give me a donation?"

"Do you take donations?" Brad asked, amused.

"Sure do. That's how I got my tent. That's how I feed my mule."

Brad hadn't seen any evidence of an animal around. "You have a mule?"

"Sure do." He pointed farther up the mountain. "A man up there keeps him for me. Keeps him warm when it's cold. Let's me sleep there, too, in one of the stalls."

Mark just shrugged as if he didn't know anything about all that.

"So tell me about the Queen of Hearts," Brad prompted, trying to get them back on the subject.

"You play poker?" the prospector asked.

"I have now and then. How about you?"

"Nah. I save what money I have. Rumor has it Amos won that mine in a poker game."

"And did he?"

"That depends on who you talk to. My granddaddy said he was an ornery old cuss."

"Amos was?"

"Yep. Didn't treat his wife none too good."

Caleb had mentioned Catherine Douglas in passing but hadn't seemed to know much about her. "What do you mean he didn't treat her well? Was he mean to her?"

"No one knows for sure. Back then women stayed because they had to." He looked Brad in the eye. "Now they don't have to."

The old man was right about that. He

couldn't imagine Emily staying in any situation she didn't want to be in. "So what about the mine?"

"The mine. The Queen of Hearts." Mickey shook his head as he leaned close to Brad and whispered, "Women have the power."

"Maybe now they do," Brad said.

"Women have the power," Mickey insisted, looking agitated.

"A woman owned the mine?" Brad asked.

The man resumed his seat with his legs crossed in front of the fire, then he stared into it as if their whole conversation hadn't happened, mumbling, "Don't know for sure. Don't know nothin' for sure."

After another twenty minutes or so of talking to Mickey, or trying to talk to Mickey, of attempting to make sense out of his ramblings and their pieced-together conversation, Brad knew he wasn't going to get anything else.

Pulling out his wallet, he took out two twenty-dollar bills and tucked them into Mickey Latimer's pocket. "There's a donation for you. Do you mind if we come back to see you again?"

"Might be here. Might not be here."

"We'll keep that in mind."

As Brad and Mark hiked back the way they'd come, neither of them spoke. Finally, in the SUV once more, Brad looked over at the reporter. "What do you think?"

"I think he's rambling, just like when I talked to him. I couldn't make much sense out of any of it."

"What do you think he meant—'Women have the power'?"

"It could be just something he picked up somewhere."

"He seemed to know a little history on Amos."

"Maybe. But maybe his memory is cloudy. Maybe he was confusing Catherine Douglas with someone else."

Brad repeated the phrase. "Women have the power."

Fastening his seat belt, Mark laughed. "That's true in my house. My life revolves around Juliet and the baby."

Thinking about acquaintances and colleagues, Brad wasn't sure he'd seen any successful marriages. However, he might not have looked very hard, either. His parents had colored the way he thought of men and women and marriage. His experience with Robin had colored it, too. But spending time with Mark and Juliet, he'd realized they seemed genuinely happy.

He'd never asked his mother why she'd had an affair or what it had meant to her. He'd never asked her why she hadn't married the man who'd come between her and his father. Brad had always believed everything his father had told him about his mom—that he and Brad hadn't been enough for her and she'd found something outside of the marriage, that she'd been selfish, only considering what *she* wanted. But as Brad grew older, he'd realized everything wasn't black or white. He'd also learned his father could be controlling and cold. Is that what had forced his mother into an affair?

He didn't like rethinking his entire life, but he understood that one of the reasons he was doing it wasn't just this trip to Thunder Canyon—he was rethinking it because of Emily.

As Mark checked his watch, he asked, "What are you doing for lunch?"

"I haven't decided yet. I was going to go back to the ranch and check on Emily."

"Why don't we stop in at the Hitching Post and get something. You might find a little taste of history there, especially when you look over the bar at the Shady Lady."

"The Shady Lady?"

"It's a painting of a woman who was rumored to own a brothel—Lily Divine. I was thinking you might run into some old-timers there who hang around and play checkers because they have nothing better to do."

"Let me give Emily a call. I'll tell her what we're up to."

When he took out his cell phone, he realized he couldn't wait to hear Emily's voice.

When Emily had found Brad's note, her heart had raced faster and she'd smiled. *It's only a courtesy note,* she'd told herself. Still, it was nice Brad had let her know what he'd be doing and that he was with Mark. After she'd dressed, poured a cup of tea and gone to the sitting room with it, her wrist ached so she'd decided to delve into some of Adele's home-decorating magazines for a distraction. But then Brad had called and seemed to just want to talk. His concern for her had made her feel all warm and fuzzy inside. After he'd described Mickey and shared some of their conversation, he'd told her he was going to have lunch with Mark and bone up on some more of Thunder Canyon's history.

Now, still paging through magazines, the sound of Brad's deep baritone echoing inside her, she decided to return to her room and look at the notes she'd taken thus far. She could try to type one-handed.

However, when she neared the dining room, she heard male voices and stopped.

"I'm going to keep that mine one way or another," she heard Caleb say.

"You know I'll do anything I can to help you, Dad."

She recognized Riley's voice.

"No one is going to cheat me out of what is rightfully mine. I've paid taxes on that land for years. No assessor ever said anything about a title not being listed."

"It's not so odd considering how records used to be kept," Riley assured him. "Every descendent after Amos Douglas just kept paying taxes as his predecessor had."

"I wonder if Amos ever had the actual deed. A lot of deals were made by word of mouth back then."

"But you *do* have the promissory note," Riley reminded him.

"Yes, I do. The question is, did Amos foreclose? Apparently the rumor about the poker game was a myth."

"Thunder Canyon is full of legends, and that was just one of them."

Instead of making her presence known, Emily quietly slipped past the dining room and went into the kitchen for an ice pack. She and Brad would have to have a conference when he returned.

When he returned.

Her heart raced faster at the thought.

Typing with her right hand, her left helping now and then, was slow going. Emily was engrossed in correcting her mistakes on the laptop screen when there was a knock at her bedroom door.

"Come in," she called absently, making another correction.

After Brad stepped into the bedroom, her heart seemed to actually sing. He was wearing jeans and a denim shirt today, with the cuffs rolled back. The shirt was open at the throat and black hair swirled there. When she'd played her fingers through that hair, it had been so soft—

"You're back," she said lightly, trying to keep the pictures from playing through her mind.

"You shouldn't be typing," he scolded her.

"You brought me along to type up notes. I can't earn my bonus if I don't do that."

"Give your wrist a couple of days to heal."

"I needed something to do."

After he crossed the room, he sat on the bed, facing her. When his jean-clad knee brushed hers, she could smell his aftershave and also the scents of the outdoors.

So she wouldn't concentrate on how much she liked the shadow of his beard line and the way his eyes darkened when he looked at her, she asked, "Did you find out anything else?"

"I don't know what's fact and what's fiction and I don't know if the prospector is senile or cryptic. But I didn't find out anything more at the Hitching Post. I told you what Mickey said about women having the power. If a woman did own the mine, none of the old-timers playing checkers there had ever heard about it.

"Women have the power," he repeated as if he still wondered what the prospector had meant.

"What power?" Emily asked, amused.

But Brad wasn't smiling. He was studying her in a way that made her blush.

"You have more power than you can ever know."

"Because a man needs a woman to fulfill his needs?" she asked softly, wishing their time in the cabin had been more than a diversion for him.

"No. Because a man needs a woman to feel like a man."

Before they'd made love, Emily might have scoffed at that, but now she knew a woman needed a man to feel like a woman, too. In that cabin, as Brad had kissed and caressed her, she'd felt beautiful and desired and feminine in a way she'd never felt before.

The hum surrounding her and Brad in its erotic field wasn't coming from her laptop. She licked lips, which had suddenly gone dry, and couldn't break eye contact.

A nerve in Brad's jaw worked. His voice was husky as he said, "I did learn a few things about Amos Douglas from Mickey that I didn't tell you about on the phone."

Trying to follow the thread of conversation, she made her lips form the word, "What?"

"It's not going to help us any, but I learned he might have been a scoundrel. There's a possibility he mistreated his wife."

"That would have been Catherine Douglas."

Brad nodded. "I'll have to take you to the Hitching Post some night. It's an interesting place—part old-time saloon, part new-time grill."

"That's the place Juliet mentioned last night. She'd waitressed there. That's where she met Mark. It must have been hard for her, being pregnant, having to work with no family around."

"I think that's why she and Mark connected." Studying her again, he asked, "Do you often think about the baby you lost?"

Emily guessed Brad was remembering holding Marissa. Maybe he was thinking about Suzette Brouchard and her child. Maybe he was contemplating the idea of really becoming a dad. He'd already missed two years of that little girl's life, according to the article in the newspaper. She wished she could put Suzette out of her head. She wished she could put Brad's lifestyle out of her head and pretend he was just an ordinary guy and they were here together getting to know each other.

Her thoughts had scrambled to another direction because the miscarriage was still painful for her to remember. "I think about that baby every day. I wonder if it would have been a boy or a girl, if he or she might have had my brown hair or my eyes, been born tiny or big." Tears came to her eyes as she shook her head.

Clearing her throat, she quickly changed the subject. "I overheard Caleb and Riley talking."

After a moment of studying her, he asked, "About what?"

"The mine. Caleb is vowing to keep it one way or the other."

"I wonder how he intends to accomplish that if I find out someone else owns it."

"I don't know. But Riley's on his side. I get the feeling he'd do anything to please his father."

"Parental approval," Brad said with a grimace. "It can be a driving force."

"Has it been for you?"

"Wanting my father's approval has always been in the back of my mind. When I was younger, I purposely took a different road so I didn't have to deal with earning it."

"But you came back to Chicago to work with him."

"Yes, I did. My mother wanted me to. I don't think she liked me being so far away and she simply pushed the guilt button several times, reminding me my father wouldn't be around forever."

"Are you sorry you came back?"

He ran his hand through his hair. "No, I'm not sorry I came back. I think she was right. I should get to know him before it's too late. But working with him, trying to fit into the vision of what he wants me to be, that's something else entirely."

After a few beats of silence, without warning Brad took her laptop from her lap and closed it.

"Brad, I have to—"

"What you have to do is give that wrist time to heal." He took her hand in his and lifted the bandage. "Did you rewrap this this morning?"

His fingers on her skin started a burning heat that didn't stop at her hand.

"No," she somehow managed to say, even though her mouth had gone as dry as cotton.

"Do you want me to rewrap it? It's kind of hard to do one-handed."

Yes, it was. If she let Brad do it, it would only take a couple of minutes, maybe not even that long.

Already Brad was slipping the small clasp

out of the fabric, laying it on top of the laptop computer. Then he was gently holding her forearm, unwrapping the stretchy bandage.

Searching for a coherent thought, Emily finally settled on saying, "What are you going to do this afternoon?"

"I thought I'd go into Old Town to the historical society and poke around."

"Want some help?"

"Sure, if you feel up to coming."

"There's nothing to do here. And if I don't think about my wrist, it doesn't hurt."

"Mind over matter?" he teased.

The bandage undone now, Brad put her hand on his thigh. Every nerve inside her rioted because she had touched him intimately there. *Mind over matter,* she repeated inwardly, as if the mantra could make his touch less volatile.

As he probed her wrist gently, he said, "It doesn't look as swollen."

"The doctor said I should only keep the bandage on a couple of days."

Brad proceeded to tuck the end of the bandage into her palm. When he began wrapping, Emily tried to pretend he was the doctor doing it. That didn't work at all.

Taking care with her and the bandage,

Brad wrapped it over and under and around her wrist. Although he did it methodically and expertly, she noticed every graze of his thumb, every touch of his eyes on her, every change of expression on his face. There were tiny lines around his eyes. His black brows drew together once when the bandage buckled, but then he smoothed it and finally attached the small metal clasp.

"There you go." His words were light, but when his gaze held hers there was no lightness there.

"Emily," he murmured as he leaned forward.

She loved the sound of her name on his lips. She loved his claiming purpose as he stood and then pulled her up, too.

When his arms wrapped around her, he said, "I don't understand this chemistry between us any more than you do."

What made them want each other? What made her eager to catch a glimpse of him? What made her want to feel him inside her again? She knew this could only be temporary. She absolutely knew it.

Yet sometimes it simply didn't matter. His kiss was possessive and took her breath away. Brad took her breath away.

Totally engrossed in their kiss, Emily jumped when the phone beside her bed rang. Brad ignored it. He knew Tess always answered it. His hands were under Emily's top now, and she anticipated the feel of his fingers on her breast. It was a delicious anticipation. Their bodies weren't quite touching, and she wanted that, too. She wanted everything from Brad.

She was pulling his shirt from the waistband of his jeans when there was a knock on her door. "Miss Emily?"

Brad swore, rested his forehead against hers and then leaned away.

"Yes, Tess?"

"Telephone. She says she's your sister."

"How does she know you're here?" Brad asked, his voice deep, desire still simmering in his eyes.

"I called home after we arrived. When they can't get in touch with me, they worry."

Instantly she guessed that was a foreign concept to Brad.

His face was unreadable now as he tucked his denim shirt back into his jeans and then went to the door. "You'd better get that. Until you're ready to go, I'll talk to Tess to see if she has those notes for me on her daughter."

Then he was leaving Emily's room and she was picking up the phone, hoping the sound of her sister's voice would bring her back to the real world, remind her that she was Emily Stanton, secretary, that Brad was her boss. When they got back to Chicago, nothing would be the same as it was here in Thunder Canyon.

Chapter Nine

When Emily skipped breakfast on Thursday morning, Brad wondered why. Her wrist seemed to be better. She'd taken off the bandage now and was using it normally. But she'd been quiet the past couple of days and he was concerned about her. Did she just want to go back to Chicago and her life? Did she want to get away from the tension between them as they slept in their rooms at night? He was aware of her, just a bathroom away, and that awareness gave him insomnia, as well as dreams he couldn't act on.

For the past two days he'd tried to learn everything he could about Tess's daughter. He'd made calls to contacts on the West Coast and he'd made local calls, too. But Annie Littlehawk's best friend hadn't wanted to talk to him. In fact, she'd hung up on him. He wouldn't stop there, of course, but he would give her a few days to think about it, to think about helping him in the search. At the moment he felt stymied on all fronts, waiting for Tildy Matheson to return, waiting for the mayor to return. Today he'd decided to see what all the fuss was about at the Queen of Hearts mine itself.

Since Emily hadn't appeared at breakfast, he went looking for her and found her in her bedroom working on her laptop at the small reading desk.

"Still organizing notes?" he asked after he'd knocked on the door and she'd called for him to come in.

"Not for the case," she said with a frown.

He saw numbers on the screen and joked, "That looks more like a budget."

Smiling, she turned away from the computer. "It is."

"Yours?"

"Unfortunately, yes."

She seemed deflated somehow, and that wasn't like Emily. Their last kiss had put another wall between them, had warned him again to keep his distance, had made him search out ways to work alone instead of working with her, but he realized he still cared what she was feeling way too much.

"What's wrong, Emily?"

Avoiding his gaze, she looked as if she was about to brush off the question, but then her shoulders squared and she pushed her chair back. "Lizbeth called me on Monday."

It was the call that had interrupted their kiss that could have led straight to the bed. "Bad news?"

Emily pushed her hair behind both ears, as though somehow straightening it could straighten out her life. "She was supposed to graduate this month."

"And now she's not?"

"She wants to change her major and go another year."

Beginning to see where this was headed, he took a step closer. "If she does that, you won't be able to start school."

"Not for another year."

"There's no way around it?"

After Emily glanced at the computer screen again, she shook her head. "Lizbeth already has more school loans than I'm comfortable with. She'll be paying for them the rest of her life. She'll have to try to get more financial aid, of course. I can't subsidize the whole year. But before she started, I told her I'd help her as much as I can, and I can't go back on my word."

"Even if that means putting your life on hold again?"

"Even if it means that."

Her expression was so troubled, he asked, "Something else is bothering you, isn't it?"

Standing, she avoided his gaze and went over to the window that looked out over fenced-in grazing land. "I'm wondering when it is going to be *my* turn. And that makes me feel so selfish."

Emily was probably the most *un*selfish person he'd ever met. "You expect too much of yourself. Blazes, Emily, you've been putting your own life on hold for how many years now? Resentment has got to go along with that no matter how much you love your sister."

Her eyes glistened as she murmured, "I don't want to resent it. I don't want to be jealous of Elaine finding a career and Lizbeth looking for hers. If I give, I want to give freely…with no strings and no regrets."

That's exactly how she'd given herself to him. But he was afraid she *did* have regrets.

In the course of their conversation, Emily had wrapped her arms around herself in a defensive posture, as if she expected judgment from him.

He crossed to her and gently clasped her shoulders. "You're Lizbeth's sister, not a saint. Don't beat yourself up for being human."

Dropping her arms to her sides, she sighed. "I was just trying to figure out if it was possible for me to go to a community college and at least start that way since my budget's going to be tight."

Before he realized what he was saying, he offered, "Let me pay for your college courses."

Emily's eyes went wide and she looked at him as if he'd suggested she do a striptease for him. "You can't do that."

He took a light tone with her. "Yes, I can. I'll be investing in your future."

Pulling away from him, she went and stood beside the desk. "I can't take your money, Brad."

"You haven't given this enough thought."

"It only takes three seconds to realize it's

a bad idea. I don't know when I'd be able to pay you back. What if I leave Vaughn? Besides, I don't want to feel like I'm taking something from a man who—"

"A man you slept with?"

Her cheeks reddened. "Yes. I just can't do it, Brad. Things are complicated enough."

"Complicated how?"

When she didn't respond, he demanded, "Tell me what's going on in that head of yours, Emily."

She bit her lower lip, then finally blurted out, "I might be pregnant! You might already be a father and need to pay child support to Suzette Brouchard. Never mind this hum between us whenever we're in the same room. That's why I didn't come to breakfast this morning."

His suspicion that she'd been avoiding him was confirmed. "Maybe we should alternate breakfasts so neither of us goes hungry."

If he'd been hoping for a smile, he didn't get one.

"What do you want to do about it?" he asked seriously. "I can finish here in Thunder Canyon myself if you want to go home."

"I won't leave a job unfinished," she protested. "That's not the way I am. I want to know who owns that mine as much as you do. And I want to talk to Tildy Matheson. I think that will be fun. It's just—"

"It's just that you don't want to be in the same room with me."

Her lashes fluttered down and then she said very softly, "I want to be in the same room with you too much."

If he took her into his arms then, he could kiss her and maybe even lead her into bed. But that would confuse her even more and confuse him, too. They were in a world away here, but what would happen when they returned to Chicago?

He wouldn't take advantage of Emily. He wouldn't pretend they had somewhere to go when they didn't. She was the kind of girl who deserved a house in a neighborhood that had block parties. She deserved a princess-like wedding gown and a man who thought highly of marriage.

Moving toward the door and away from her was one of the hardest things he'd ever done. For whatever reason, Emily Stanton was like a shooting star that had exploded into his life. He didn't want either of them to get any more burned than they already had.

At the door, he stopped. "I think we both need an excursion."

Now her lashes came up and she lifted her gaze to his. "What kind of excursion?"

"We need to see this infamous gold mine that could put this town on the map. I also want to visit Annie Littlehawk's best friend. Do you want to go with me?"

She seemed to give the idea much thought. They'd still be together and that sexual hum between them would be ever present. But they would have the mine and Renée Bosgrow to focus on.

A smile finally spread across Emily's face. "That sounds like a great idea."

"How soon can you be ready to leave?"

"I'm ready now."

Ten minutes later they were in the SUV, driving down Thunder Canyon Road. They were heading toward the access road to the mine when Brad's cell phone rang.

"Vaughn here," he said as he kept his eyes on the road.

"Brad, it's Suzette."

The artificial sweetness in her voice turned his stomach. "You should be talking to my lawyer, not to me."

"Look, sweetheart, maybe the lawyers are the wrong way to go."

His jaw clenched when he heard the endearment. "Your lawyer started this whole thing."

"I realize that now. But I understand what this must be doing to your reputation."

"It's not doing anything to my reputation, Suzette. I'm not even in Chicago."

"Not in Chicago? Where are you?" Some of the sweetness had left her voice.

"I'm on a case, and in a minute or so the static is going to interfere with our signal. So you'd better tell me why you called."

"I just wanted you to know we can settle this whole thing without the DNA testing or results."

"I had the DNA sample taken before I left Chicago."

There were a few moments of hesitation and then she went on. "Even so. You know those results can prove you're the father."

He was about to protest heartily when she continued. "I'm sure we can come to an equitable settlement so you don't have to go through the embarrassment of the whole process."

"There won't be any embarrassment for

me. I know what the results are going to say, and I have no intention of settling—not now, not later."

"But, Brad—"

Brad didn't know if the mountains were interfering with the signal or the weather or simply the particular location he was driving through. But one moment she was there, the next moment she wasn't.

After a futile, "Hello? Suzette?" and no answer, he reclipped the cell phone onto his belt.

Knowing Emily had heard every word, he glanced over at her. "She wants to settle."

"And you don't."

"That's right."

He'd discovered that the man Suzette had lived with ever since Brad and she had broken up had gambling debts. He had a feeling Suzette had been bankrolling her boyfriend and now her modeling money had run out. He wasn't going to be a ticket to the easy life for the two of them.

After his call, Emily went silent. Brad wished she could trust him, could trust his word. But after what he'd let happen in the cabin, he could see why she was still in doubt. The thing was, the situation with Emily had never happened to him with another woman. He'd never before felt that overwhelming desire not only to be intimate with but to protect and look after a woman. He didn't understand the inclination at all.

Following directions Caleb had given him, Brad veered onto the gravel road that led to the mine. It had obviously not been used much until the past few months. It was rutted, uneven and felt like an amusement-park ride as they bumped over it.

As he rounded a pile of boulders Caleb had given him as a landmark, he spotted the mine entrance cordoned off by yellow tape about a quarter mile down the road. No Trespassing signs were posted, and Caleb had told him the police did periodic drive-bys.

Brad slowed to get a good look around. Seconds later a shot rang out!

Brad braked fast, rocking them both against their seat belts.

"What was that?" Emily asked. "A backfire?"

Another shot broke the air and grazed the hood of their car. Brad no longer looked around for explanations. In a sputter of mud and a skidding U-turn, he headed for the way they'd come.

When he pulled over after the next bend, Emily asked, "What are you doing?"

"Sit tight," he ordered. "Keep the windows closed. If you see anyone, if anyone approaches you, hightail it out of here."

"And what are *you* going to be doing?"

"There's a pickup parked near the mine entrance. I'm going to get the license number. No one shoots at me and gets away with it."

"You're crazy!" She grabbed his arm. "Don't go back there. You could get hurt."

He saw worry in her eyes for him again, and in spite of the situation it made him smile. "I'll be back. Five minutes tops."

"I am *not* sitting here alone. I've been stranded in a cabin in a snowstorm, rescued by helicopter, shaken up by a horse and now shot at. That's enough for me. It should be enough for *you*."

Cupping her chin in his hand, he kissed her hard. "I'll be back."

Then he left the keys in the ignition, locked the door and ran to the side of the road under the cover of firs.

As Emily sat waiting, she tapped her foot, peered in every direction and constantly looked over her shoulder. She should drive off and leave Brad stranded here, but she'd never do that. In fact, if she found out he was in trouble, she'd drive right into it.

Each minute ticked by slowly. She counted them until finally Brad was running toward the SUV and knocking on the window for her to let him in.

She leaned over and unlocked the door.

Climbing inside, he started up the SUV and drove them as far as Thunder Canyon Road. Then he pulled over again and took hold of his cell phone.

In the next few minutes, he called 911 and told the dispatcher what had happened, giving him the license number of the pickup truck. After also giving the authorities his name and cell number, he ended the call.

Glancing at Emily, he asked, "Are you okay?"

No, she wasn't. Each one of his kisses affected her more than the last. Each touch of his hand, each one of his smiles, made her heart turn over. But she wouldn't let him know that. She wouldn't let him know she wanted her dream with him.

"I'm fine. But do you think we can stay out of trouble for the rest of this trip?"

At her tone, he laughed out loud. Then he

undid his seat belt, leaned close to her and kissed her.

Brad's kisses were never the same, and this one was no exception. After his lips brushed over and pressed to hers, she parted her lips. But he didn't take advantage of that. Instead he nibbled at the corner of her lip, then ran his tongue over her upper lip, and she felt as if she'd melt into a puddle on the car floor.

Her moan must have told him that because she heard the low growl in his throat. She saw him prop his arm on the back of the seat to take some of his weight as he leaned in. She could feel his body heat and his desire as well as his hunger. It didn't scare her; it made her want. She wanted Brad again in a way that was so elemental, she didn't even understand it. She wanted Brad in a way that would fill up her life and fulfill her dreams. She wanted Brad...and she wanted more. Although she'd given him the impression she wanted to return to Chicago, she liked being here with him. She more than liked being here with him.

When his tongue finally slid into her mouth, she pressed against him with a yearning that had never been a part of her before this trip. She might have fantasized about

Brad, but the reality was so much better than any fantasy. The reality was more than she'd ever imagined.

Her jacket was unzipped, and Brad's hands slipped underneath it. She could have protested. She could have shifted away from him. But that was the last thing she wanted to do. Her minutes with him were precious. His touch was something she'd never forget. When his hand moved over her breast, she could recall vividly every moment of their time in the cabin. One afternoon had been so erotically sensual, she didn't know if anything could top it. One night had been so safely protective, she never wanted to forget it, either.

Did Brad act like this with the models, actresses and account executives he dated? Was she only a diversion because they were away from the city?

Her questions changed the kiss even though she hadn't voiced them.

He pulled away but didn't take his gaze from hers. "What are you thinking?"

"You make me feel as if I'm the only woman in the world. Do you do that with all the women you date?"

Slowly he leaned away from her and

shifted back into the driver's seat. Staring straight ahead, he admitted, "You've gotten under my skin, Emily, and I don't know what to do about it. Because I'm not what you need."

"What do I need?" she murmured, almost afraid of his answer.

"You need a man who knows how to commit himself to one woman. You need a man who wants a gold band around his finger as much as you do. I spent my adult years doing everything I could do to stay disentangled from a woman's life. You need a man who will become totally involved in yours."

"You never want to get married? You never want children?"

When his gaze swung back to hers, she saw his answer. He made it definite when he responded, "It's never been in my game plan."

"You might already have a child," she reminded him.

"That's the thing, Emily. You can't even believe me when I tell you I'm not the father of Suzette's child. So I'm definitely not a man you want in your life."

He was deciding what she needed and what would be best for her life. That hurt her, and her hurt turned to anger. "I think it's more than that. I think I'm not the caliber of woman your father would approve of and that bothers you."

His jaw clenched. "That has nothing to do with this."

"I think it has everything to do with this. You're the boss and I'm your secretary. You live in a high-rise condo, ride in limousines and travel wherever you want. I'm just a nobody from Chicago who's never even been on a camping trip."

"You're mistaken."

She kept silent because she knew she wasn't.

A police SUV turned onto the access road, its lights flashing, and pulled up beside Brad.

Turning to Emily, Brad repeated, "You're wrong." Then he exited the SUV to tell the policeman what had happened.

Tears came to Emily's eyes, and she simply didn't know what to think anymore.

After Brad finished a brief but thorough conversation with the lawman, the officer drove toward the mine. Brad passed a backup police car zooming toward the mine and he wondered if Emily was ever going to talk to him again that afternoon. Whatever attraction they felt for each other was at an all-time high. As he headed toward Old Town, the life he'd led up to this point seemed to play in front of his eyes. He wouldn't give Emily false hope that his opinion of commitment and marriage would ever change.

All that said, he wished she'd talk to him. He wished they could recapture their earlier camaraderie.

To try to start dialogue between them once more, he mentioned, "This best friend of Annie's might shut the door in our faces."

"You said her name's Renée?" Emily responded stiffly.

"Yes."

Silence once more pervaded the car until Brad parked at the curb. As they walked up to the brick stoop, Emily kept her distance from him. No matter. His lips still burned from their kiss and his body hadn't altogether recovered. At the door there was no bell, but Brad let the brass knocker thump twice.

A teenage girl answered the knock. For the most part her hair was brown, but there was a circle of red on the crown of her head that looked chemically induced.

She was tall and thin and her green eyes

glanced from him to Emily quizzically. "My mom doesn't have any more of those tin cups to sell," she said, assuming that's what they were there for.

"Tin cups?" Emily asked.

"Yeah, you know. With the prospector painted on the side. It'll be another week until she has more done."

Apparently Renée Bosgrow's mother was making an item tourists liked to buy. "We're not here for tin cups," Brad said. "Are you Renée?"

Now the teenager's eyes narrowed and she grew wary. "Who wants to know?"

He extended his hand to her. "I'm Brad Vaughn, and this is my assistant Emily Stanton. Tess Littlehawk asked me to find her daughter, and since you were her best friend, I need to talk to you."

"I was her best friend before she took off. But I told you on the phone I don't got nothin' to say."

"Even if you don't, I'd like to speak to you for a few minutes."

Renée took a step back. "Why?"

"Because I want to explain to you how it feels when someone you love goes missing."

Her expression changed a bit, only a bit,

but Brad saw it and took advantage of it. "Renée, Tess Littlehawk has a hole in her heart because a child she gave life to can't be found. I don't know why Annie left, and I don't need to. I only know her mother needs to hear her voice. It's been three years, and she has the right to know whether she's alive or dead."

"Dead? Annie can't be dead."

Emily's quiet but steady voice asked gently, "Do you know that for sure?"

After a long pause, Renée shook her head. "No, I don't. I don't know where she is now."

"But she told you where she was going when she left?" Brad guessed.

As the wind played with Renée's hair, both the brown and red strands, she crossed her arms, plucking at the red sleeves of her sweater. "I promised not to tell anyone where she went. We were like sisters. I can't break my word to her."

"It's been three long years," he pressed. "You said you don't know where she is now. She's probably not anywhere near her destination of three years ago."

The logic of that seemed to sink in. "Did Mrs. Littlehawk tell you why she ran?"

Tess had written pages for him, revealing

all. "She told me Annie hated being a cleaning woman's daughter and that she was dating boys Tess wasn't comfortable with."

"Comfortable with? She grounded her when she snuck out to see Ronnie."

"She didn't believe she should be dating yet," Brad said, standing up for Tess.

"Annie was a looker. She had boys all around her. Dating isn't something you suddenly decide you can do because you're old enough."

Brad realized that if he had a daughter that's exactly what he would do. He'd keep her locked up until a boy finally met his approval. However, he wasn't going to argue with Renée about when girls should date. "Tess was afraid she'd get in trouble."

"You mean her mom was afraid she'd get pregnant."

"Yes, I imagine she was afraid of that, but she was also afraid she'd get into a car with an older boy who had been drinking. Annie had done that and that's why she was grounded."

Staring down at the toes of her sneakers, Renée mumbled, "Annie wanted to be a model or an actress."

Now they were getting somewhere. That

usually meant a trip to California. "She went to Los Angeles?"

Renée's eyes widened as if he'd just caught on to what made the world spin. "What makes you say that?"

"Give me a little credit. Isn't Hollywood the land of dreams?"

Looking across the street to a row of houses that was similar to the one she lived in, Renée admitted, "She didn't go to Hollywood."

When it seemed she wouldn't give them more information, Emily found a way to touch her on a different level. "Tess just wants to find out if she's alive and well. Think about *your* mother. What if she didn't know where to find you for three years."

Renée suddenly said again, "She *didn't* go to Hollywood."

"Then where did she go?" Brad asked, realizing again how good Emily could be in investigative work.

Minutes seemed to tick by until Renée shuffled her sneakers on the stoop and jammed her hands into her jeans pockets. "She used the computer at school and went to this chat room that a modeling school in L.A. set up. She couldn't afford the fees to go to the modeling school, but she got to be friends with another girl there—in the chat room. That's when she started making plans."

"Plans to go to L.A.?" he prodded.

"No. This girl—I think her name was Lena—lived in San Jose. Annie saved every penny she could for a year, and Ronnie took her to Bozeman. She bought a bus ticket to California."

"You know this for certain?"

"Yeah. Ronnie told me after he got back that day. He said she was crying and laughing all at the same time and couldn't wait to leave."

"Is this Ronnie still in town?"

"No. His brother lives in Portland. He went up there to live with him after he graduated."

"You don't know this Lena's last name?"

"No. I don't even know if Lena is her real name. You know how chat rooms go."

Unfortunately he did. He just hoped Lena was a girl who wanted to go to modeling school and not a predator preying on teenagers with dreams.

"Thank you, Renée. You've helped us a lot."

"You're probably right and Annie's not still in San Jose." That thought seemed to salve Renée's conscience. With that, she shut the door.

"What do you think?" Emily asked, looking up at him now.

"I think she told us all she's going to tell us. After three years, there's a possibility Annie's not in San Jose. But there's also a fifty-fifty possibility that she is. I have a place to start."

When a strand of Emily's hair blew across her cheek, he couldn't keep himself from brushing it away. His thumb on her cheek sent a jolt through him. "Emily, look. About what happened in the car—"

She shook her head. "Don't worry about it, Brad. I know where you stand. I won't misunderstand anything that happens between us."

In other words, she accepted their attraction to each other for what it was—chemistry.

Why didn't that make him feel better?

Chapter Ten

That evening, Caleb wouldn't take no for an answer and neither would Adele. The Montana Mustangs, a band they both enjoyed, were playing at the Hitching Post this one night only. They insisted Brad and Emily shouldn't miss the event.

As Brad rounded the SUV and opened Emily's door, she wondered why this felt like a date when it wasn't. Caleb had decided to drive his own car, but she wished he hadn't. Conversation would have been easier with the four of them.

"You just don't see a sky like that in Chicago," Brad said with appreciation as he helped her down from the SUV.

He was still holding her hand, and she didn't let go of his as she looked up at the black velvet sky, the almost full moon and the thousand pinpoints of stars. "The sky might be the same in Chicago. We just forget to look at it."

His gaze dropped to hers, and when he studied her lips, they both knew what he was thinking. Instead of kissing her, however, he slammed the SUV door, then he tucked her hand into the crook of his elbow as they walked up the street and then took a step up onto the wooden promenade.

The Hitching Post sported a wild-west-style false front and looked like an old-time saloon. After Brad opened the heavy wood door, Emily could see that the floor was hardwood and at one end of the restaurant there was a long curving bar. Framed photos from the 1880s hung on the walls. The Montana Mustangs were set up near the bar and dance floor at the far end of the room.

After they hung their coats on a long rack, Brad leaned down to her ear and his breath whispered across her cheek. "Caleb said this used to be a saloon. It was renovated many years ago and turned into a restaurant, but you can see the history all around."

Emily saw history all right. There was a painting above the cherrywood bar, and the woman looked almost nude! She was a voluptuous blonde with a wicked grin, wearing a gauzy fabric draped over her breasts so that she wasn't entirely indecent. The effect definitely did not portray a proper lady.

A cash register stood at the end of the bar, and a matronly woman with silver-streaked hair worn in a topknot sat on a stool there. Almost smack-dab in the middle of the dance floor stood a contraption Emily didn't recognize.

"What's that?" she asked Brad.

As he eyed it, he grinned. "That's a mechanical bull."

"What do you do with a mechanical bull?" she asked almost to herself.

Just then the band member on guitar stepped up to the microphone. "Ladies and gentlemen, our bull-riding competition is about to start before our first set."

"There's Caleb." Brad's hand went to the small of her back as he guided her toward a table near the wall.

Caleb was grinning from ear to ear. "What do you think, Brad? I may be too old to get my bones shaken up, but you aren't. The prize is three hundred dollars."

Placing a restraining hand on her husband's arm, Adele shook her head. "Don't let him goad you. That machine's not much safer than the real thing."

"Adele, honey, you worry too much."

"If I remember correctly, when Riley was eighteen, he broke his arm falling off one of those things," Adele maintained with a stern look.

At the thought of Brad getting hurt, Emily gazed up at him. "You're not going to try it, are you?"

"Don't you think I'm in shape?" he asked with another grin that made her feel tipsy even without a drink. Remembering his naked body all too well, she decided his good shape wasn't part of this equation.

"You might be in shape, but that doesn't mean you won't get hurt."

"A bit of risk spices up life."

"A little risk can put you on crutches."

Laughing, Brad pulled out a chair for her. After she sat, he lowered himself onto the chair next to her.

"The Montana Mustangs bring that thing along for entertainment value," Caleb explained. "The bartender's always glad because he sells more drinks while the clientele work up the courage to go for the money."

Emily knew if Brad rode the mechanical bull, he wouldn't be riding it to go for the money. In fact, she wasn't sure why he would do it. Just for the thrill?

As the Mustangs played lively country music, one by one men with Stetsons, snap-button shirts and boots tried the mechanical creature. Most only lasted a few seconds. One or two almost made it to the end of the ride. A lean young man in his early twenties took his turn, and Emily winced as he was tossed onto the straw-strewn floor and landed on his shoulder.

He was slow to get up and she shook her head, muttering, "Stupid, stupid, stupid."

Brad's chair scraped against the floor as he stood. Leaning close, he rested a hand on her arm. "Watch how this *should* be done."

"Brad," she called as he strode toward the man-made machine that she believed should be declared illegal.

The band started a new tune as everyone

clapped and Brad climbed onto the "bull." With a grinding whir it started slow and then sped up until Emily was clenching her hands together, her knuckles white. She couldn't believe Brad was holding on!

At least, one minute he was holding on and the next…he was on the floor, facing the stage rather than the bull!

The whole room applauded because he had stayed on a fair amount of time. But as he rose to his feet and seemed to be unharmed, Emily's relief was short-lived because he motioned to the bull again, indicating he wanted another go-around.

He was out of his mind. That was *her* verdict.

However, when Brad climbed on board again, Emily realized she shouldn't be surprised. Brad Vaughn was a man who conquered his mountains and always got exactly what he wanted. She didn't like the idea of him getting shaken sideways and backward and upside down again, but she had to admire his courage. His ride started again, and this time he not only stayed on, but as he raised one arm over his head, his body seemed to move in rhythm with the machine. To everyone's amazement, he lasted on the bull until the ride wound down and the machine turned off.

Most of the patrons in the Hitching Post got to their feet and applauded, including Caleb and Adele. Emily joined them, clapping as loudly as she could.

Returning to the table with a wide grin, Brad accepted the slaps on the back, the offers of free drinks and the praise for a ride well-done.

Emily was about to add her kudos to the rest when a woman in tight black jeans, a bright red shirt with buttons open to show cleavage and a white cowgirl hat approached Brad at the table. "You're new around here, cowboy."

"Just visiting," Brad answered nonchalantly with a smile.

"How about the first dance? Now that you've conquered that thing, they're going to move it away so everyone can have some real fun."

The fun this woman spoke of made Emily see green. She'd never realized she had a jealous streak. When she and Warner had been dating, they'd kept it low-key, secluded, away from the public. She realized afterward he'd wanted their relationship kept secret because he hadn't wanted to be seen dating a secretary in the firm. Even so, when she'd seen women with him in the law offices, she'd never felt this desire to scratch their eyes out. This woman in the cowgirl hat was entirely too bold, brazen and proprietary as she laid her hand on Brad's arm and stared up into his eyes with a coy look meant to lure him to dance with her.

Emily simply couldn't stand it. "He's dancing the first dance with me," she blurted, amazed at what had come out of her mouth.

At Brad's amused expression, she wanted the floor to swallow her up.

"Is that true?" the cowgirl asked, giving Emily the once-over. She eyed the white western shirt with embroidery, the ironed blue jeans, the flat leather shoes.

"That's true," Brad admitted as the bull was wheeled away, straw was swept up and the band started up again.

"Maybe I'll just have to cut in," the cowgirl stated.

"I'm not sure you want to do that," Brad responded with a wink at Emily. "She might look delicate, but I hear she boxes in her spare time. It would be a pleasure to dance with you," he said with a consoling smile, "but I promised I'd dance with Emily tonight, and I don't break a promise."

The cowgirl looked from one to the other and then she gave a little shrug. "The good ones are always taken. See you around, cowboy."

Emily knew her cheeks were bright red. Her heart was racing so fast she could hardly breathe.

She was ready to sink into her chair and keep quiet for the rest of the night when Brad's arm went around her shoulders. "We told her we were going to dance so we'd better get out there and do it."

Couples were already on the dance floor. But they weren't standing in traditional dance poses, and Emily didn't understand the steps they were executing.

"I don't know how to do that," she whispered as Brad walked her to the dance floor.

"It's the Texas two-step and it's real easy to catch on to. Just follow me. You'll be fine."

Follow him. She was beginning to think she'd follow him anywhere.

At first Emily felt totally ridiculous. She didn't know how to dance the Texas two-step. She didn't know how to dance! Her feet seemed to want to go in every direction but the right one. But then Brad's arm tightened around her, his feet seemed to direct hers and they were moving around the circle behind another couple, amazingly keeping in step. Finding herself breathless, she realized it was because she could feel Brad's heat, inhale his scent, lean into his strong body. Everything about him shouted "fantastic male," and she wished she could get past the dizzying sensations of dancing with him, being with him… loving him.

When she almost tripped, Brad caught her. "Are you okay?"

No, she was definitely not okay. She was irrevocably in love with Bradley Vaughn. Not falling in love. Already fallen.

"Just learning the steps," she mumbled as they got into the rhythm of it again and she tried to pull the blinds on the realization that seemed life-altering.

They had finished the first dance when Emily felt a twinge in her side and then some cramping. Familiar with the rhythms of her body and its shifts and changes, she pulled away from Brad's arm. "I'm going to freshen up."

He cocked a brow inquisitively.

She simply smiled and slipped away, finding the short hall that led to the ladies' room.

Five minutes later, Emily washed her hands at the sink and wanted to cry. Her reaction was totally irrational. She should be glad she'd gotten her period—absolutely thrilled. It meant she wasn't pregnant. A baby now should have been the last item on her agenda. Yet she realized she hadn't yet bought a pregnancy test because she'd been nurturing the idea of a baby, getting used to it, anticipating a bond with Brad that would last a lifetime.

As she looked herself in the eye in the mirror, she saw the futility in all of it. Getting pregnant was the worst reason to have a connection to a man. It was the worst reason to think about a relationship. She'd known that for years. Her love for Brad had to rise or fall on its own merit. If he had feelings for her, she couldn't attach strings to them. If he had feelings for her...

She knew they would change and evaporate once they returned to Chicago.

With her purse under her arm, Emily practiced a smile in the mirror and returned to her table to pretend to enjoy the Mustangs for the rest of the night.

As she approached Adele and Caleb, she saw Brad talking to a uniformed officer. It was the policeman from the SUV that had arrived after Brad's 911 call from the mine.

By the time she reached Brad's side, the officer had moved away and was threading his way through the crowd.

She took her seat and waited for Brad to take his. When he did, she asked, "Did he catch whoever shot at us?"

"Yes, they did. After I called, they notified surrounding towns. Law enforcement in Livingston spotted the truck. It turns out there was a warrant on the driver for an assault charge. The good guys won this one."

"Because of you. Not just anyone would have had the courage to get that license number."

"You didn't see it as courage at the time," Brad joked.

"Yes, I did. But I was scared and you weren't. At least if you were, you didn't show it."

"I've had a lifetime to practice hiding what I feel."

When they'd arrived in Thunder Canyon, his guard had been solidly in place. But while here, she'd seen it slip now and then.

Caleb ordered another round of drinks, interrupting their conversation. As the Mustangs played, all Emily wanted to do was talk to Brad privately. They couldn't do that here. After munching on peanuts and sipping her club soda with its twist of lime, she danced the Texas two-step with Brad again.

When the song ended and the band began a slow ballad, Brad turned her into his arms. "Maybe we can catch our breath on this one."

She doubted that. She absolutely couldn't let Brad hold her. She couldn't give in to her love for him because she knew it had no place to go. "I'd like to go back to the ranch," she said seriously.

His smile slipped away and he released her. "If that's what you want." His expression had gone stony and she explained, "It's not that I don't want to dance with you. I do. But we need to talk. Can we go?"

He relaxed some. "All right. Let's find our coats and I'll tell Caleb and Adele we're going back."

"The Mustangs too much for you?" Caleb asked as Brad brought her her jacket and she slipped it on.

"The Mustangs were great," Emily assured him. "But I have some notes I want to work on."

Caleb's brows arched and he looked as if he didn't believe her. "Don't forget to collect your winnings," he reminded Brad.

Brad nodded. To Emily he said, "I'll just be a minute."

Waiting by the door while he spoke to one of the band members, she studied the picture of the Shady Lady again. After Brad joined her, they went outside.

"Did they give you a check?" she asked.

After a short hesitation, he responded, "The Mustangs donate time and money to juvenile diabetes. The lead guitarist has a daughter with it. So I told them to donate the prize money to that."

It was becoming harder and harder for Emily to reconcile her old image of Brad with the new one that was forming.

As soon as they'd climbed into the SUV and fastened their seat belts, Brad asked, "Do you want to wait until we get to the ranch to talk or do you want to talk now?"

She didn't want to wait. She really didn't have that much to say. "I'm not pregnant. I got my period tonight."

After a few moments of silence, Brad

started the engine, pulled out of the parking space and drove onto the main road. They'd driven about a half mile when he commented, "I suppose that's a relief to you."

"Isn't it a relief to you?"

"Actually for the past few days I was thinking of the possibility of being a father."

"Only the past few days?"

"Have I ever lied to you, Emily? Or misled you?" His voice was gruff with a hint of anger.

She thought about the months she'd worked for him and had to say, "No, you haven't."

"Then why would I start now?"

She held on to what she once believed about him because she was safer with that barrier between them. "Maybe because Suzette Brouchard could take you to court and use me as a witness. You want to make sure I'm on your side, and if you convince me to believe you—"

"Stop! We've spent almost two weeks together. Some of that time in very intimate contact. Just how do you think you would feel if I told you I thought *you* were lying to *me*?"

"I have no reason to lie."

"And neither do I."

Confused by her love for Brad, his reputation as a love-'em-and-leave-'em bachelor, feelings that she couldn't understand and she couldn't push out of her heart, she kept silent. Anything she said right now would only make matters worse. She knew if they didn't soon leave Thunder Canyon, her heart would be irreparably broken and she'd never be able to piece it back together again.

For the next few days, Brad tried to keep everything businesslike between him and Emily. His body yearned for satisfaction with her again, and he told himself it was simply a physical need that he could deny or take care of himself. But when she was beside him, taking notes, asking questions or just listening, he resisted the urge to take her into his arms. He resisted the urge to admit he felt closer to her than he'd ever felt to anyone.

While they waited for the mayor's return, as well as Tildy's, Brad left no stone unturned. After conferencing with Mark again, he went through piles of issues of the *Thunder Canyon Nugget* as far back as they went. He also spoke to the prospector again and with anyone else who might know anything about the history of Thunder Canyon, the Queen of Hearts mine or Amos Douglas. But he came up empty.

He and Emily were poking around at the historical society Tuesday afternoon when he got a call on his cell phone from his father. As Emily studied exhibits, he took it in an alcove.

"What in God's name are you still doing there?" Phillip Vaughn demanded.

Not for the first time in his life, Brad realized he didn't like answering to his father. "Look, Dad, if I could wind this up now, I would. If I'm going to take over the agency someday, you're going to have to learn to trust me."

"As long as I'm still the head of the firm, I call the shots."

That was the problem. His father was still head of the firm, and Brad wondered now if he would be until his dying day. It wasn't just answering to his father that bothered him, it was the type of cases that Vaughn Associates dealt with. He was still waiting for word from a California contact about Tess's daughter. What he would prefer was going out there himself. Then again, he had to rely on the people he trusted.

Glancing at Emily after hanging up, he

saw she was standing in front of a display of a mannequin wearing a faded red satin dress that was trimmed with black lace. Ropes of fake pearls around the mannequin's neck, along with a black ostrich feather in its hair, accented the outfit.

"These clothes belonged to a woman named Lily Divine," she mused as he came to stand beside her. "You said she's the Shady Lady in the portrait."

"That's what I heard. She was supposedly the madam of a whorehouse."

Emily studied his expression, her concern now with him rather than with the artifacts. "Is everything okay?"

"My father expected us to return to Chicago by now. I was trying to explain for the third time why we were still here."

"I guess he didn't listen the first time," Emily said with a smile.

"If my father *ever* listened the first time, the world would stop spinning on its axis."

"You're not friends, are you?" she asked.

"Friends? Hardly."

He couldn't quite wrap his mind around that idea. He didn't think Phillip Vaughn was a friend to anyone, yet he did have his cronies who dined with him at the club and expensive restaurants, who played tennis with him. Brad had known true friendship with James, but since then it had eluded him—until this trip with Emily. It was odd, but he felt as if they'd become real friends.

"Are you and your mother friends?" he asked.

"Absolutely. I mean, she was a parent and all, gave us rules and guidelines, made sure we lived up to our potential. But she was always there to talk to. She helped with makeup and went to the movies with us. She's still a big part of my life. So are my sisters and brother, and I can't imagine it any other way."

The museum was shadowy, with not a lot of direct lighting. Brad gazed down into Emily's pretty face and watched her green eyes sparkle like emeralds. "We're so different, you and I."

"I guess we are in some ways. But in others..." She shrugged. "I think we're a lot alike."

Her conclusion surprised him. "How?"

"We work the same way. We analyze and think things through. We're both perfectionists. We both have a few walls, but deep down inside we just want to be accepted for who we are. And on top of all that—" she grinned up at him "—I think I've even grown to like Thunder Canyon and Montana."

Her expression was so mischievous, so genuine. He cupped her chin in his palm and raised her lips to his. When he kissed her, she didn't pull away.

Until the beeping of his cell phone intruded.

Aware that a docent might interrupt them any second, Brad broke the kiss, gave her a wry smile and answered the phone.

"Vaughn here."

"This is Elma Rogers, Mayor Brookhurst's sister. He's back. He said he'll meet you at the archives room anytime you'd like."

Brad glanced at Emily. "How about in fifteen minutes?"

Twenty minutes later, if the mayor was surprised by Brad's impatience, he didn't show it. Unlocking the door to the archives room with his key, he turned the knob and pulled the heavy door open.

The mayor was in his fifties and dressed casually. A portly man with a handlebar mustache, he wore trousers with tan suspenders and a pale blue, long-sleeved shirt. The top of his head was bald and his graying black hair fell over his collar in the back.

"I'll have to stay with you," he said to them now in an apologetic tone. "These are all documents that need to be protected, and nothing can leave this room without my okay. Understood?"

"Understood," Brad agreed, eyeing stacks of ledgers, books and boxes. "Do you know if this is in any type of order?"

The mayor motioned to the left wall. "All I can tell you is that those ledgers are being entered into the computer."

"Do you know the years?"

"Eighteen eighty to 1920, but not all of them are there. Our last archivist hadn't finished going through the boxes to find more. And, of course, there are those that were destroyed by the fire in the late 1800s and the flood more recently. From what I understand, there are gaps and holes. But you're welcome to look through all of it if you're careful."

Brad and Emily spent the next three *days* looking through all of it. They went through every box, every musty page, every book, newspaper and bound volume. They found some ledgers from the late 1800s. There were a few volumes from between 1890 and 1910, but none listed a transaction concerning the Queen of Hearts mine.

Finally at the end of their third day, Brad shook his head. "Tildy Matheson was supposed to return home yesterday. Let's call her and see if she'll let us come over this evening. She might be our last hope. It just doesn't seem possible if Caleb Douglas's ancestors owned this mine, as well as the mineral rights, that there's not a record of it somewhere."

"We're used to the tech age. Recording deeds was very different back then."

"Maybe. But I'm not ready to give up. I'll buy you dinner at the Hitching Post and we can call Tildy from there."

When Brad called Tildy from the saloon, she warned him not to eat dessert. Her sister had sent homemade oatmeal cookies with her, and Emily and Brad were welcome to share them.

Tildy Matheson lived in an old Victorian house. When she opened the ornate old door graced with a stained glass window, she was smiling. Tonight she wore a brightly colored blouse and slacks as she motioned them inside. "I'm so pleased you called. My family doesn't want to hear about old times. It's nice to talk to younger folk who do. Come on in."

Tildy's house was situated in Old Town, and Emily glanced around the interior, seeing at once that it was charming. Tildy obviously loved flowers. Her chintz sofa was covered with blue and green ones, and the drapes were made of the same material. The windowsills were hardly visible under small plants.

Crossing to the window, Emily took a closer look.

"African violets," Tildy explained. "I just love them. My neighbor took care of them for me while I was gone."

A Tiffany floor lamp brought rainbowed light into the room. Many of the furniture surfaces, including the bookshelves and the end tables, were covered with framed photographs.

"I put water on for tea. It should be ready now. I'll get it and the cookies."

As Emily helped Tildy in the kitchen, the woman chattered all the while. "I was just finished napping when your young man called. Traveling always tires me out for a while."

"Did you have a nice trip?"

"A wonderful trip. I appreciate every minute I have with my family. At my age I never know what the next day will bring. I just wish I could get around better. I don't go upstairs much anymore. Last year my niece insisted I turn my sewing room into a bedroom on this floor so I didn't have to do the steps. She was right. I certainly don't want to fall. But I miss not being able to wander into every nook and cranny of my house."

Emily admired Tildy's bone china painted with pretty pink blooms as she set three cups on a tray. "It was my grandmother's. It *is* pretty, isn't it? She had a fondness for flowers, just like I do. Just grab that can of cookies over there on the table."

After Tildy led Emily back into the living room, she spotted Brad studying the photographs.

"Some of these look quite old," he noted as Tildy settled herself in a fern-covered wing chair.

"They are."

After they all balanced their saucers and their teacups, Tildy asked, "Now, where would you like me to start?"

"Do you know Caleb Douglas?" Brad

asked, setting his cup on the coffee table. Emily knew he didn't much care for tea.

"Everyone in Thunder Canyon knows Caleb Douglas."

"He's trying to prove his family owns the land where the gold mine's located."

"That gold mine. Such a hubbub over a few nuggets of metal."

"Mark Anderson told us one of your ancestors knew Catherine Douglas."

"Oh, yes," Tildy admitted proudly. "That would have been my grandmother." She pointed to the photographs on the bookshelves. "See that end photograph on the first shelf? That's my grandmother and Catherine."

Brad's gaze met Emily's and he stood, crossing to the shelf to pick up the photograph.

"That was taken in front of the town hall," Tildy explained.

Brad brought the picture to Emily so she could study it, too.

"We've been trying to find records from back then," Emily offered.

"It's easier to find stories," Tildy responded.

"What kind of stories?" Brad asked.

For the first time all evening, Tildy hesitated. "The kind of stories that are passed down in a family."

Emily could see Brad's focus intensify as he set the picture on the coffee table and seated himself once more. "Can you tell me about them?"

"I thought you wanted to know about the history of Thunder Canyon. There's a legend—"

Before she went off on a tangent, he intervened. "Caleb's ancestors are part of the history of Thunder Canyon, aren't they?"

"Yes, but there are some things people don't talk about much."

"Such as?" he prodded.

Gently Emily asked, "Isn't it better for true history to come out rather than something that's made up just because it sounds better?"

"I suppose you're right." Tildy's gaze met Brad's. "My grandmother used to tell me stories. She wasn't the type of woman to spread rumors."

"What stories did she tell you?"

Again Tildy hesitated. Finally she admitted, "That Amos Douglas wasn't the pillar of this community everyone thought he was.

He abused his wife, and Catherine was afraid of him."

Tildy's statement landed in the room with a thud, and Emily realized the Douglases might not be what they seemed. She held her breath and waited for Tildy to tell her story.

Chapter Eleven

"I guess I should start at the beginning." Tildy's gaze swerved from Brad to Emily. "I'm still not sure I should be telling you any of this."

"If it relieves your conscience any," Brad interjected, "I had already heard the rumor that Amos abused his wife."

"Where did you hear that?" Tildy asked.

"The old prospector, Mickey Latimer."

After Tildy thought about that for a few moments, she gave a shrug. "Stories came down to him, too, but like me he kept quiet. Now I don't think he remembers what he tells people and what he doesn't. What else did he say?"

"Not much else. When I asked him about the gold mine, he would just repeat, 'Women have the power.'"

"I don't know about that. Women in general had a tough time of it back then. And many times they had to hide their true character."

"I don't understand," Emily said.

"My grandmother and Catherine Douglas were friends—*confidantes,* as they called it back then. Catherine told Grandma things she never told another living soul. She put up a good front, and few people saw through that. My grandma always told me, though, that Catherine lacked the courage to change her life."

"You mean by leaving Mr. Douglas?" Emily asked.

"Precisely." Tildy pointed to the picture on the bookshelf. "Over and over again my grandmother offered to take her in, but she simply said Amos would hurt my grandma and her family if she did that. Catherine wouldn't bring that harm on them. She was probably right. Amos was a scoundrel. He was wealthy and had a lot of power in these parts. And there wasn't an ounce of kindness in him. The way he got that gold mine was immoral."

"So he did own it?" Brad asked.

"It wasn't that simple. I don't know if you've heard talk about Lily Divine."

"Her picture hangs in the Hitching Post." Brad looked totally intrigued now.

Tildy wrinkled her nose. "Yes, it does, and I'm not sure how all that came about. But I do know she wasn't a prostitute or a madam."

"What *was* she?" Emily prompted.

"She was a lady trying to find her way in a world of men. She was smart and she was one of the few women to own land. *She* owned that mine."

At their stunned silence, Tildy continued, "She had also inherited a house from a madam. There were prostitutes around, of course, and lots of times the johns mistreated them. When that happened, Lily would nurse them back to health again."

"I can see how she'd get the reputation of being a madam," Brad muttered.

"The women in town knew the true story. But as I said, women weren't as vocal then as they are now. Pretty soon other women besides prostitutes came to her. Women who were being mistreated. But times got tough, and in order not to lose the hotel she had built across the street, she had to mortgage the gold mine property. She'd known Amos Douglas had his eye on the abandoned Queen of Hearts mine. She knew she couldn't get a loan through the bank, but she might be able to get one from Amos and she did. Only there were strict terms involved and when she missed *one* payment, he foreclosed."

Brad's gaze met Emily's and they thought about the promissory note that Caleb held in his possession.

"One payment and that old buzzard took the deed for the mine from her," Tildy related again indignantly.

"So Caleb *does* own it."

"It would seem so." Tildy sighed. "But I haven't told you the rest of the story."

Already on the edge of her chair, Emily found the history fascinating.

"One night, after all that happened, Amos went on a particularly bad rampage and Catherine got the brunt of it. She was pretty badly beaten. She didn't want to go to friends or relatives because she was afraid Amos would hurt them in some way, too. Even knowing what happened with the mine, she went to Lily because she thought she was her last resort. And Lily didn't turn her away. That woman had a kind heart. She nursed Catherine back to health and tried to convince her to leave Amos. But so many women in that position do the same thing—they stay. Catherine said she had to go back home. She didn't feel she had a choice. She told Lily she'd be grateful to her till her dying day, but then she returned to her husband."

"How sad," Emily murmured.

"I'll say it was. When I was younger, I would go through that old trunk up in my attic and think about the life women had back then."

"What's in the trunk in your attic?" Brad asked.

"Oh, I guess I didn't tell you. When Amos died, Catherine became rich in her own right. Of course, she left everything to their son—everything except her personal possessions. Her will stipulated that they go to my grandmother. So up in the trunk I have some of her clothes, pictures like that photograph over there, combs she wore in her hair. I keep her antique jewelry in my jewelry box, and I've worn it all my life. My grandmother gave it to me when I was a teenager. I'd be glad to get it if you'd like to see it."

"I'd love to see it," Emily said enthusiastically.

"This trunk," Brad mused, "you say it's in your attic?"

"Yes, it is. I've been wanting to give it to the historical society, but my niece hasn't found time to bring it down and I certainly can't get to the attic anymore."

"Would you mind if Emily and I look through it?"

With narrowed eyes, Tildy studied them both closely. Then she smiled. "You seem like upright young folk to me. Go ahead. By the time you return I'll have the jewelry out and more hot water for tea."

After Tildy showed Brad and Emily to the stairs, she instructed them, "If you go into the smallest bedroom, last one on the left, you'll see a closet. Just open the door and the stairs to the attic are in there. Be careful. They're narrow."

"We'll be careful," Brad assured her.

In a matter of minutes Brad and Emily found their way to the attic door. At the foot of the stairs, Brad flicked on the light switch.

He went up first and led Emily to a corner where an old trunk sat. The attic smelled musty, and there was a layer of dust across the trunk.

"No one's been up here in a while," Brad said as he examined the latch.

The trunk looked to be made of wood with leather stretched on top. It had hand-sewn edges. "Amazing." Brad ran his hand over it. "The historical society would treasure this."

After Brad lifted the lid, they peered inside. The trunk was about five feet long and three feet wide. Inside, clothes and photographs were tumbled together as if in its trip up the stairs everything had gotten mixed up. On the left side of the trunk, the material lining the inside was torn.

"Maybe someone could restore this," Emily murmured.

Seeing tears other places, Brad shrugged. "They might have to reline it."

Seated on the floor across from each other, they went through everything piece by piece. Emily held up a blue dress that had faded to purple. Its neckline was low cut, its sleeves full and puffy.

"What do you think?" she asked with a coy smile.

"I think you would have been the belle of the ball."

Brad's voice was low and deep and sent a thrill up her spine. There had been so much distance between them since she'd told him she wasn't pregnant over a week ago. Each day her love for him was growing and she wanted to be close to him, not have a wall between them. Yet that wall was protecting her.

"What's wrong?" Brad asked.

"Nothing."

"Emily?"

"I was just thinking about...us."

"And the fact that you're not pregnant?"

She nodded.

He looked as if he were going to lean toward her then. He looked as if he might kiss her. Instead he turned toward the trunk once more. "We'd better finish with this or Tildy will think we stole everything and escaped through the window."

As they sorted through each photograph, they studied the old clothes, the faces, the buildings in the background. Emily found a hand mirror of tarnished silver, a lady's parasol and a flimsy pouch made of silk hidden in the folds of a dress. Both the dress and the purse had once been green, but now they were faded and yellowed with age. The bottom corner of the purse was torn.

About to lay it back inside the trunk, Emily

heard something crackle. She ran her thumb and forefinger over the silk.

"What is it?" Brad asked.

"I don't know. I think there's something inside."

Prying open the drawstrings, she carefully slipped her hand in and pulled out another photograph. It was a cameo portrait of Catherine Douglas. Emily recognized her from the photograph downstairs. "She was a beautiful woman."

"And in the end apparently she got everything Amos owned."

"I wonder what happened to her? Tildy didn't say."

Emily laid the photograph on top of all the others. "I guess we should repack the trunk."

Carefully folding one of the dresses, Emily laid it in the bottom and folded another on top of it. The billowing skirt raised dust. Her fingers brushed the inside of the trunk as she lifted her hand to rub her nose, but her watch caught on the material of the lining and ripped it more.

"I'm ruining a historical treasure," she moaned.

"That lining is falling apart from old age."

Examining the new tear, worried about it, Emily thought she glimpsed something a different color than the wood. Hoping she wasn't going to do more harm than good, she eased her finger under the torn material. There was an envelope sticking to the wood. She didn't want to tear that, too, and she carefully extricated it.

Brad had been studying the photographs, but now he glanced up. "What do you have?"

"I don't know. It must have slipped behind the torn lining."

The envelope was old, brittle and yellow. Emily expected it to be a letter, maybe one Tildy and her mother had missed when they'd looked through everything. Who knew how long it had been lost inside the lining?

Reaching her hand down along the lining once more, she felt something else. It was thin, but she could feel its edge. Slipping her hand farther inside, her fingertips touched paper. Drawing it out, she saw it was a photograph of a man with a bushy mustache and a cowboy hat shading his brow. She had no idea who the man was, but wondered if it could be Amos Douglas. She showed it to Brad, and while he was studying it she opened the flap of the envelope and pulled out the sheet of paper inside. It was folded in half.

She saw *Queen of Hearts*. She saw *mineral rights*. Then she saw the transfer notice still in the envelope. When she spotted the line with the name of the landowner, she gasped. It was Lily Divine.

"What's wrong?" Brad asked.

After Emily handed him the deed, she perused the transfer notice and the date. In amazement she said, "Catherine Douglas transferred the mine back to Lily Divine!"

"Let me see that," Brad demanded.

After he examined all of it—Catherine's signature, the official embossing mark—he gave a whoop of success. "We did it, Emily! We *found* the deed."

Before she knew what was happening, he'd taken her into his arms and hugged her. She lifted her mouth to his and he lowered his to hers. The musty attic seemed to be heaven on earth. Brad kissed her with the pent-up passion he'd been suppressing for days, and she kissed him back with the same overload of desire she'd been denying. Neither seemed to be able to stop the onslaught of needs unsatisfied as they kissed harder and deeper and longer.

Then Brad was breaking away, looking down at her as if he didn't want to end the kisses but knew he had to.

"I'd better be careful with this." He waved the deed in front of them. "It survived this many years—I don't want anything to happen to it now."

No, of course he didn't.

"Emily?" his expression was suddenly sober.

"What?"

"This means we'll be leaving Thunder Canyon." He seemed to be waiting for her reaction.

The idea rolled through her and she felt shaken by it. Everything would change when they returned to Chicago. Everything. She wouldn't even be his secretary anymore.

Forcing a bright smile, she said, "You succeeded. Your father will be thrilled."

But that didn't bring an answering smile from him. "Yes, I guess he will be. But Caleb won't. He just lost a gold mine. Let's put all this away and go down and tell Tildy what we found."

Ten minutes later, they were showing Tildy the document.

"Land sakes!" she exclaimed, then sank

into her favorite chair. "Lily Divine's the owner. If that don't beat all. My eyes aren't too keen anymore, but I think that's the year Catherine Douglas died."

"How did she die?" Brad asked.

"There was an epidemic of pneumonia that year. One day she was perfectly healthy, a week later she was dead."

"Maybe she had the deed transferred and never had the chance to give it to Lily," Brad surmised.

"She probably thought she was righting wrongs done to both of them. If Amos swindled Lily out of the mine to begin with, and Catherine was grateful for the care Lily had given her, it makes sense."

"The deed will have to be authenticated, of course." Brad added, "But I think we found the true owner of the Queen of Hearts gold mine. Do you know if she has any descendants?"

"She does," Tildy said with excitement. "Lisa Martin, her great-great-granddaughter."

"Do you know her?" Emily asked.

"No, believe it or not, we've never officially met. I know who she is. She has a pet-sitting business." Tildy examined the deed again. "This is so exciting. She just inherited a gold mine."

"Don't go spreading that rumor yet," Brad said with a wink. "The first thing I'm going to do is find an expert to have the deed authenticated. If it's as old as I think it is, then we'll inform Lisa Martin that she just inherited the Queen of Hearts."

"I wouldn't want to be in *your* shoes," Tildy said to Brad. "Caleb Douglas is going to be mighty put out about this, and that's an understatement."

"Caleb Douglas already has enough money and holdings to keep his descendants happy for a few generations. *If* they don't go through it like water."

"A man like Caleb Douglas always wants more," Tildy warned Brad. "Would you like to save the jewelry for another time?"

"Yes. I think we'd better be going. Lisa Martin is going to owe you a great debt."

"I didn't do anything."

"You could have tossed that trunk a long time ago."

Tildy gestured to Emily. "*She's* the one who had the good sense to look inside the lining. That tells me she's not deceived by outside appearances. You'd better hang on to this one," Tildy advised Brad with a wink.

Knowing she was blushing to the roots of her hair, Emily turned away and picked up her coat. Brad would be letting go of her, not holding on to her. She knew that in her soul.

Less than a half hour later, Brad and Emily were closeted with Caleb in his den. Brad handed him the deed with the transfer notice.

"This is a fake," Caleb boomed.

"I don't think so," Brad countered evenly. "Somehow it had slipped inside the torn lining of a trunk that dates back to the gold-mine era."

"You can't know that."

"Tildy assures us she inherited that trunk from her grandmother. She cherished everything that's inside it."

"Then why's it still in her attic?" Caleb blustered, looking as if he wanted to tear up the document in his hands.

In a flash, Brad took the document from Caleb. Emily knew he'd seen the same intent in Caleb Douglas's eyes.

"I'll hold on to this for safekeeping. Once we have it authenticated, we'll know what to do next."

Paling, Caleb looked trapped. "Lily Divine was a prostitute."

"That's not the story Tildy tells. She got that reputation because she helped prostitutes and watched over them like a mother hen, protecting them from abusive johns, caring for them when something bad happened. Apparently Lily Divine was a woman of character, ahead of her time. If this document pans out, her great-great-granddaughter, Lisa Martin, will inherit the gold mine."

"No," Caleb interrupted forcefully. "That mine belongs in our family."

"Your great-grandfather took unfair advantage of Lily Divine when she mortgaged that property to him. He didn't deserve it."

"You have no right to decide who deserves anything." Caleb's gaze went to the deed in Brad's hand and then his expression changed. "Look, Brad, why don't you and I talk about this reasonably. If you forget you ever saw this particular piece of paper, I'll make it worth your while...very worth your while. Anything you want—a share in the ski resort, shares in one of my other holdings or maybe you'd like five hundred thousand dollars in cash."

Although she was appalled by Caleb's

offer, Emily held her breath waiting for Brad's response.

Brad's shoulders straightened, his jaw locked into place and he seemed much taller than six foot three when he responded. "You can take your money and your resort and your stock shares to your grave with you. I don't want them."

Carefully he folded the deed and transfer notice, slipped them back into the envelope and slid it into his shirt pocket. "I'm going to call a courier and make sure this gets into the right hands tonight. You'd better accept the fact that the Queen of Hearts gold mine simply isn't yours. Emily and I will be flying out tomorrow."

As Emily studied Caleb Douglas, she realized he looked like the most unhappy man she had ever seen. She was so proud of Brad and his integrity.

After she followed him out of Caleb's office, she laid her hand on his arm to tell him so. When he turned toward her, he still looked angry over Caleb's offer.

"I'm so proud of you."

"For not taking the money?"

It was so much more than that. "No. For being determined enough to find that deed, for telling Caleb where he could put his money, for handling all of it so well."

His expression gentled then as he slipped a hand under her hair. "I haven't handled *you* well. Something about you makes me forget common sense. We never should have had sex without protection. I never should have let you go horseback riding."

"I think we were both in denial, trying to pretend something hadn't happened when it had. I was as much to blame as you were."

Now both of his hands were in her hair and he was cupping her head, looking down at her. "Blame has nothing to do with this anymore. The chemistry between us is just too explosive to ignore, and maybe we should give in to it this one last night."

He could have started kissing her and carried her upstairs to a bedroom, sweeping her away. They both knew she was susceptible. But he wasn't doing that, and she suddenly realized that if he said he wasn't the father of Suzette Brouchard's child, she could believe him. Brad was a man of integrity and a man of honor, and tonight she wanted to love him one last time.

With a shaky smile she asked, "Your bedroom or mine?"

* * *

Forty-five minutes later, Emily sat in her bedroom brushing her hair. The shower was running, and she knew in a few minutes she and Brad would be together, at least for tonight. He'd made a call to a courier service in Bozeman after they'd left Caleb's office. Five minutes ago, she'd heard the courier's van drive away from the Lazy D ranch. In a few days, they'd know if the deed was authentic. Her instincts told her it was.

When the shower stopped running, she stopped brushing. Her suitcase was packed except for the clothes she'd left out to wear tomorrow for the trip home. Thank goodness her period was over. Thank goodness she had this one last night to pretend her dreams could come true.

As she laid her brush on the dresser, the door to her room opened and Brad stood there naked. This time she didn't turn away. This time she let her gaze roam over him, appreciating the muscles, the lines of his taut stomach, the curling black hair. The longer she stared, the more aroused he became.

"My bed's bigger." He held out his hand to her.

Placing her hand in his, she wasn't immune

to the heat rippling up her arm nor the desire in his eyes. Leading her through the bathroom, he then let her precede him into his bedroom. As she quickly glanced around the room, she noticed he'd turned down the bed and placed packets of condoms on the nightstand. When his arms wrapped around her, he brought her close. He'd dried off, but his chest hair was still damp from his shower, as was the hair on his head. She could feel his arousal through her robe. She could feel the beat of his heart.

With his index finger under her chin, he lifted her face to his. "Are you sure?"

She'd never been more sure of anything in her life. She loved Brad Vaughn and tonight she was going to show him just how much. "I'm sure," she murmured.

When Brad kissed her, Caleb Douglas and the deed and Tildy and Thunder Canyon all fell away.

"I can't get you off my mind," Brad breathed between kisses. "I remember that afternoon in the cabin, the night I held you, and I feel different than before I came here."

"In what way?" she whispered against his lips.

"I'm not sure. I just know my life isn't

going where I want it to and I'm going to change directions."

Then all thoughts of direction and work and Chicago were very far away.

Stepping back, Brad's hands went to Emily's belt. He untied it and her robe fell open. He didn't hurry to rid her of it. Rather, his hand brushed over and around her breasts, making her crazy with need. She reached out to him and ran her hands down his chest, over his stomach.

When he sucked in a breath, she smiled, and he laughed. "You've learned you have power, too."

"Not much."

"More than you know."

Sweeping her off her feet, he lifted her into his arms and carried her to the big bed, where he gently lowered her. She scooted over on the sheet and he came down beside her, facing her. Tonight he didn't hurry any of it. He took his time getting to know every inch of her. She took her time getting to know every inch of him. Where before they'd been frenzied and too hungry to wait, now Brad prolonged each caress to give her the most erotic pleasure she'd ever experienced. She explored his muscled thighs with her hands and lips and tongue, making him as crazy with need as she was.

Finally he admitted, "I'm beyond my limit, Emily, but I want to make sure you're ready."

"I'm beyond ready."

Smiling, he slid his hand between her legs to make sure, then took her lips with a searing kiss that burned through her whole being. No matter what else happened or didn't happen between them, she'd remember this night forever.

After Brad tore open the condom packet, she helped him roll it on. She did it slowly, teasingly, and he groaned.

"Just you wait," he growled.

Then he rose above her and entered her with such slowness, she wanted to cry. She was waiting all right—waiting for him to fill her. Finally he did.

In that moment, time stopped.

She felt whole and loved and cherished.

When he started moving inside her, pleasure began building higher and higher until it was beyond any sensation she'd ever felt, brighter than any stars she'd ever seen, more encompassing than any feeling or desire that had ever overtaken her heart. Brad's final thrust tossed her over the mountain into free fall. His cry of release said he'd followed her.

She held on to him and he held on to her, and their landing was gentler because they had each other. With Brad's arms around her, with his body still connected to hers, her breathing slowed and so did his. Eventually he raised himself on his elbows and looked down at her.

"I'm glad we have all night. That wasn't nearly enough."

Emily knew exactly what he meant. But she also knew tonight would have to be enough, because when they returned to Chicago everything was going to change.

Chapter Twelve

On Monday morning, Emily reported to work early, not knowing exactly what to do. If she was going to be promoted, should she start working on anything that had come in while they were gone? On the other hand, she had yesterday's notes on Caleb's case to type up. That could take her a good part of the morning.

To her delight and dismay, Brad came in early, too. The night she'd spent with him in his bed had been heaven. Still, yesterday morning they'd awakened to the alarm, hurriedly dressed to drive to the airport on time and then flown away from Montana. Brad had said nothing about their night together and neither had she. He'd been perfectly clear about it from the outset. On her part, however, her love had grown along with her passion, and now she hated the thought of letting it go—letting *him* go.

This morning he'd greeted her and then had enclosed himself in his office. Now that door opened and he beckoned to her. "Emily, can I see you?"

Her heart pounded as she picked up her notepad and pen and went inside. "You won't need that," he nodded to the notepad. "I think you'll remember everything I have to tell you." He smiled at her then, but it was a forced smile and didn't light up his eyes.

"What is it?"

"I spoke with Jack McCormick this morning and explained how helpful you were in Thunder Canyon. I asked him to think about taking you on in a training capacity. He's willing and said he could use the help from someone as capable as you are."

"He's never worked with me."

"No, but he looked up your evaluations and he considers my recommendation a golden one. He knows I'm hard to please. So, as soon as you have the notes typed up on Thunder

Canyon, finish up whatever else you think needs your final touches and tomorrow morning report to Jack."

"Tomorrow morning?"

"Is that a problem?" Brad asked.

About a ton of them, she thought, realizing this would be the last day she'd be working with Brad, the last day she'd spend any appreciable time with him.

She impulsively asked, "How would you like to have dinner at my mom's apartment tonight? It's a welcome-back dinner for me, and I'm sure she'd like to include you."

His gaze held hers. "Why are you inviting me?"

"It's a celebration for the work we did together, finding the real owner of the mine. It's also a thank-you for the promotion. We won't be...seeing each other much after today."

She knew she was only prolonging the inevitable, but she was so head over heels in love with Brad, she couldn't quite let go.

He hesitated long enough to tell her he was thinking about refusing, but to her surprise he finally responded, "All right. That sounds nice. What time should I be there?"

"Around seven?"

"Seven's good. I need the address."

Quickly she scribbled her mother's address on the pad, then tore the sheet of paper off and handed it to him. As he took it, she gazed at his long, strong fingers, remembering how he'd taken her out of herself as she'd welcomed him, remembering how tenderly they'd stroked her. Desolation overtook her because she knew he wouldn't be touching her in that way again.

"Can I bring anything?" he asked.

"No. Just yourself." Then she forced a bright smile and said, "I'll get those notes on Caleb Douglas finished as soon as I can," and went back to her own desk.

When she sat in her swivel chair, a tear rolled down her cheek and she knew she'd been an absolute fool to invite him to dinner.

Picking up the phone, she called her mother to tell her Brad was coming tonight.

Carrying the box wrapped with light blue paper decorated with a premade darker blue bow, Brad rang the doorbell to Mrs. Mary Stanton's apartment.

The intercom came on and an older female voice asked, "Yes?"

"Mrs. Stanton? It's Brad Vaughn. Emily invited me to dinner."

"Yes, she told us you were coming. Come on up. Everyone can't wait to meet you."

That wasn't what Brad wanted to hear. It had been a mistake to accept this invitation. But every time he thought about Emily going to work for Jack, his gut clenched. Every time he thought about looking out into her office and not seeing her there, he realized how important she'd become to his day-to-day work regime. When she'd issued the invitation to dinner, he'd known he should have refused, but when he was with her he felt taller, smarter and a better man. He told himself he'd merely woven some kind of glorified web about them since Thunder Canyon, and reality would come crashing through any moment.

It hadn't happened yet.

Stepping into the elevator, he pressed the button for the fifth floor. As the elevator rose, he had no idea what to expect when he reached the Stanton's apartment. Who else would be at this dinner besides Emily and her mother? Would Mrs. Stanton sense there was more than a business relationship between him and her daughter? A relationship he knew he had to sever, for Emily's sake if not for his.

When he rang the doorbell to apartment five-twelve, he was surprised when a man opened it—a man maybe a few years younger than he was. He looked a lot like Emily only his jaw was more square, his eyebrows thicker and he was much taller.

"So *you're* Brad Vaughn," he concluded in a voice that told Brad he wasn't overly pleased Brad had come to dinner.

Brad extended his hand. "And you're...?"

"I'm Eric Stanton, Emily's older brother." He gave Brad's hand a perfunctory shake. "She told us you were coming. We received the wine you had the store send us. It's expensive stuff."

"I thought your mother would enjoy a chardonnay."

"Mom likes wine that tastes like fruit juice, but she'll try it because you sent it. Come on in."

In a matter of minutes Brad was introduced to Eric's wife and two daughters, as well as Lizbeth and Elaine. He searched the living room, which was charmingly decorated in rose, peach and green with small porcelain figurines on top of most available surfaces.

Lizbeth must have noticed him glancing around. "Emily's in the kitchen. She's putting the finishing touches on dinner. Come on, I'll introduce you to Mom."

One of Brad's best traits was mingling and making conversation with strangers. He'd been doing it since he'd earned his MBA and worked on Wall Street making cold calls to potential clients. However, tonight he felt out of his element. Maybe he cared about what these people thought about him. That idea totally unsettled him.

Lizbeth was a pretty coed with light brown hair and a slim figure shown to its advantage in tight jeans. A good fourteen years older than she was, fatherly thoughts came into Brad's head—the jeans shouldn't be so tight, the blouse should button up a little higher, she shouldn't be wearing so much makeup.

"Is that for Emily or Mom?" She motioned to the package in his hand.

"Emily."

"I thought you'd say that." She grinned as they went through the dining room, with its table set in white ironstone china. "She's nuts about you, you know."

His quick glance made her toss her hair and shrug her shoulders. "Well, she is. And I hope you feel the same way about her. She doesn't deserve to get hurt again."

They stopped outside the closed door to the kitchen. "No, Emily doesn't deserve to get hurt," he said evenly. "No one does. But sometimes that's hard to prevent."

"Are you saying you're not serious about her?" Lizbeth's eyes were wide.

"I'm saying I shouldn't be having this conversation with you. We don't even know each other."

"Well, she told us all about you—what you do and all."

"What I do?"

"Yeah, being a private investigator. She said you tracked down that deed like a hound dog on a trail. She bet there wasn't anything you couldn't find. Like I said, she's nuts over you. But don't tell her I said that. She's pretending it's nothing special that you came to dinner, but she wore her best slacks and favorite blouse. So that's hogwash."

To change the subject, he focused on Lizbeth. "Emily mentioned that you were going to spend another year in college."

"I'm changing majors. It's hard for me to decide exactly what I want to do."

"You mean this isn't it? You still aren't sure?"

"I think I'm sure. CPAs make pretty good money, but I imagine it can get a little boring. I figured I'll try it."

Suddenly Lizbeth's airy attitude really annoyed him—not only that she was poking into his and Emily's personal lives, but that she was taking advantage of her sister and didn't even seem to mind it.

"You do know Emily wants to go to college herself?"

"Someday."

"Not some faraway day. Sometime soon."

His tone startled Lizbeth. "Well, I guess. She's getting older and all."

"She wants a worthwhile career just like you do. But she's put her life on hold and she sacrificed so you and Elaine could get through your schooling before she did. So before you tie her up for another year, maybe you ought to be sure about what you want to do."

Lizbeth looked at him as if he'd suggested she become an oceanographer instead of a

CPA. Then she became defensive. "Emily's never said she didn't want to help me."

"Of course she hasn't. She's a good sister. She's reliable and she's dependable and she loves you. She sincerely wants to help you. But how long should she put herself second or third or fourth?"

After a few moments, Lizbeth cocked her head. "What happened to you guys in that cabin?"

Now he was the one who was surprised. "I don't know what you mean."

"Emily said you didn't even know each other before you left for Montana. And here the two of you are—she's swooning because you're coming to dinner, and you're…you're trying to put everything right for her."

He did want everything to be right for Emily. And as far as what happened in the cabin…

"We were put in a basic survival scenario at the cabin. We got to know each other very quickly."

"True character comes out in that kind of situation and all?" she jibed.

"Maybe so. Then we had the opportunity to work on an unusual case. It didn't seem unusual when it started, but Thunder Canyon is very different from Chicago. I think we both appreciated the differences."

"Emily never wanted to camp or go to Montana, but now when she talks about it... She got pictures developed and the scenery is gorgeous. She said she didn't just look at it, she felt it."

"She's right about that."

"You know something?" Lizbeth asked rhetorically. "Eric was all set not to like you, but I think you're okay."

With that declaration she pushed open the swinging door into the kitchen, and Brad followed her inside.

As soon as Brad stepped into the room and saw Mary Stanton, he knew she was a lady. Taller than Emily, she wore her salt-and-pepper brown hair in a sleek French twist. Her sweater and pants were an impeccable navy blue, in contrast to her daughter's pale pink.

When she extended her hand to Brad, she smiled. "Hello, Mr. Vaughn. Thank you for keeping my daughter safe while you were in Montana."

He looked for an underlying meaning to her words and found none. "She kept me on my toes."

Mrs. Stanton laughed. "I imagine she did. Emily can be quite creative. She's been telling me about her new promotion. I never thought of my daughter as a private investigator."

"She'll make a good one someday, if that's what she wants."

Mary looked from one of them to the other and capped Lizbeth's shoulder. "Let's you and I go see if everything on the table is where it's supposed to be."

"Mom, you had me check it—"

Nudging her youngest daughter into the dining room, Mary let the swinging door shut behind them.

"Hi," Emily greeted him brightly. She'd been tearing lettuce leaves and now she dried her hands on a towel and hung it over the handle on the oven. "I hope my family hasn't been too...daunting."

"Not daunting. Interesting."

"That they are. What have you got there? The wine's great. I told you you didn't have to bring anything."

He handed her the present. "This is for you. Sort of a Montana-wasn't-what-we-expected and a promotion gift."

Just looking at Emily—her silky brown

hair, her wide green eyes, her slender figure in the pretty pink outfit—he was aroused and ready for another night in the bedroom. But that was the whole problem. Emily wasn't a torrid-affair kind of woman. She deserved a hell of a lot more.

Her fingers trembled slightly as she detached the bow from the gift, and he wondered if he truly affected her the same way she affected him. Taking care with the paper, she only tore it where she had to, then she set it aside on the counter and stared at the box.

"Oh, my gosh. You didn't!"

"I felt responsible for the other one being damaged."

"I took it to the camera shop so we could take the film out and salvage it. It was going to be expensive to fix it, so I was just going to wait a while. But this—"

Taking the lid from the box, she pulled out the camera in its leather case. Unzipping the protective pouch, she took out the piece of equipment carefully. "Oh, my gosh. It has *everything.*"

"That's what the man said. So now there's no excuse for you not to take the very best pictures and submit them to magazines for consideration."

"You want me to be a P.I. *and* a photographer?"

"I want you to be whatever you want to be."

Her gaze met his, then she set the camera on the counter with the wrapping and gave him a hug. Dressed in a polo shirt and khaki slacks tonight, he could feel every one of her curves against him. He could also smell her perfume and breathe in her shampoo. He needed her too damn much. It would have been easy to kiss her. It would have been easy to prolong the hug. But neither would have been the right thing to do.

Leaning away, he said, "It's supposed to do as well indoors as outside. You might want to take a few of your family."

"More than a few. I bet Eric will want to borrow it for the kids."

"And you'll let him?"

"Maybe. But I have the feeling I'm going to be protective of this for a while. Thank you so much, Brad. You didn't have to do this."

"I know I didn't. That's why I wanted to."

"I want to show Mom, and we have to get supper out before it burns. I hope you like meat loaf."

He hadn't had meat loaf since he was a kid and his mother made it for him every Wednesday night. "Meat loaf sounds great."

Seated at the dining room table with her family, he realized the meal felt like a Norman Rockwell Thanksgiving. Dinner conversation was lively. The problem was, every time Brad gazed into Emily's eyes, he couldn't look away. And it seemed neither could she. They were seated across the table from each other, but that didn't diminish the magnetic pull he felt toward her.

Surprised he found it easy to talk to this family, Brad entered some of the conversations. Lizbeth went on about college and the people she knew there, and Elaine recounted colorful anecdotes. Eric was the only one who was particularly quiet. His wife and two children didn't seem to notice as they ate their meal with gusto, and then the two little girls ran into the living room to watch a DVD. When it was time for dessert, Emily disappeared into the kitchen to help her mother and Elaine. Lizbeth went to the china cupboard in the corner and removed cups and saucers, the sugar bowl and the creamer.

While she was doing that, Eric leaned

closer to Brad and asked, "So, this trip to Montana—was it all business?"

"It was business," Brad answered without elaboration.

Eric gave him a penetrating look. "Emily went on and on about visiting a couple and a baby. You know, don't you, that she wants a passel of kids someday."

Brad hadn't known that for certain, but he'd guessed. When he'd seen Emily with Marissa, he'd known motherhood was in her nature. Just the way she related to her sisters proved that.

"Emily will make a wonderful mother." Brad knew that in his soul.

Frustrated he wasn't getting more out of Brad, Eric continued poking. "She said she's not going to be working with you anymore. Is that true?"

"That's true. She's going to train with a senior private investigator. If she likes the work, she can get her license."

"You think she's really cut out for that?"

"One thing I don't do is underestimate Emily. If she decides that's what she wants, nothing will stop her. And she'll be good at it, too."

When Eric studied Brad, as if gauging his

sincerity, Brad became irritated. "I'm looking out for Emily's best interests, too."

Finally Eric backed off. "I just wanted to make sure of that. She's tough and smart but she's more vulnerable than anybody knows."

Brad knew that's why he had to cut this off now. He couldn't say their last night together had been a mistake. It had been too intense and fulfilling to be a mistake. But that last night was going to make everything said and done between them now even harder.

After dinner, Brad stayed a while longer. It was the polite thing to do. Finally, though, he said his good-nights and then he asked Emily, "Walk me out?"

Not hesitating, she followed him to the door and out into the hall.

Her smile slipped from her lips as she looked up at him. An awkward silence settled between them. Finally she murmured, "Thank you again for the camera."

After a very long moment, he said, "You deserve the best, Emily, the best of everything." He took a step away from her.

"I'm not going to see you again, am I?" she blurted out.

"No, not like this. It's best for you if we

don't. I don't have anything to give you. One day you'll meet a man worthy of you."

"I've already met a worthy man. You have more to give than you think. But *you* have to believe that. Up until now, you thought you *were* your reputation, and I'm not sure you considered being anything else. In Montana, I saw so many sides to you that you keep hidden."

Every word was going through him like a lance...because he could feel the truth in what she said. But she wanted a family, children—the very things he'd avoided all his adult life.

"Your life is about family. Mine isn't."

"Yours could be, too, if that's what you wanted. You think because your parents divorced, because you were shuttled back and forth from one to the other, that you don't know how to be a husband or a father. But I think you're wrong. With Juliet and Mark's baby..."

He couldn't let her go on with this. He couldn't let her think there was hope. "I held Marissa for fifteen minutes. That's not being a father."

"It's the *way* you held her," Emily protested with certainty.

"You're seeing what you want to see."

"And you're denying what you think you have to deny."

In spite of himself, he couldn't keep from touching her one last time. Reaching out, he trailed his thumb across her cheek and felt her tremble in response. He wanted to kiss her so badly that nothing in the world seemed to matter—not his career, not his money, not his reputation, not anything he'd valued before. If he kissed her, he'd be taking advantage of her. If he led her on, he'd be worse than the irresponsible playboy she once thought he was.

"I have to go." He dropped his hand to his side. "Tomorrow you'll start working for Jack. If you put your heart and soul into it, you'll be great."

"I think my heart and my soul are busy thinking about something else right now."

"Forget about me, Emily. Tell your mother and your sisters and brother I had a great time."

Walking away from her, he stopped halfway to the elevator. "And use that camera for the best pictures you've ever taken."

Fortunately when he pressed the button on the elevator, it opened immediately. He stepped inside, wanting to get a last glimpse of Emily. However, before he could glance down the hall, the doors whooshed shut and she was gone.

His heart told him to stay. His head told him to leave.

He *always* followed his head.

In spite of her stern lecture to herself—that Brad had to go his way and she had to go hers—Emily cried on and off throughout the night. She'd seen the real Brad in Montana, a loving, caring man who could make a commitment, say vows and live a happily ever after if he chose it. Happily ever after wasn't a fairy tale or a dream, it was a choice. When you had the right person beside you...

She'd found the right person, but the problem was *he* didn't think he was the right person. There was nothing she could do about that.

When she went into work the next morning earlier than usual, Brad wasn't there yet and she was thankful for that. She had to empty her desk, pack up her personal belongings and take all of it down to Jack's office.

She was removing an extra pair of shoes from her bottom drawer when Brad came through the door followed by a beautiful blonde and an older man in a three-piece suit. A younger man in a suit and tie tagged behind.

Brad opened the door to his office as he said to the blonde, "My lawyer has the DNA report. We'll be finished with this in five minutes."

Seeing Brad this morning was like a punch in the stomach, and Emily found it hard to take a deep breath. She'd lectured herself before coming to work that she might run into him. And she told herself that in the days to come that was a very distinct possibility, too. He and Jack often worked together. They consulted on cases. The gossip mill in the firm would keep her apprised of exactly whom Brad was seeing and whom he wasn't.

Sinking into her desk chair, she realistically thought about all of that for the very first time.

She couldn't do it. She simply couldn't do it. She couldn't work in the same firm, hearing news about him, seeing him in the hall or even having to deal with him. She loved him too much for that.

There was no way she could accept this promotion. No way at all.

Studying the three boxes on her desk, she decided to take them to her car and head home. But first she would type up a letter of resignation.

With tears in her eyes, she knew the only solution to loving Brad was leaving Vaughn Associates for good.

Chapter Thirteen

Brad stood in his father's office, relieved the meeting with his lawyer and Suzette Brouchard had gone so well. Of course, when the proof was printed in black and white—

"So Brouchard admitted she and her boyfriend were just trying to get money out of you?"

"She said it was her boyfriend's idea. With the test results, knowing with one hundred percent certainty that I'm not the father, what else could she say? They thought if they put enough pressure on me, especially through the media, they could get a settlement before the DNA testing results came in."

With a shake of his head Phillip Vaughn sighed. "Women."

Right now Brad didn't want to hear about his father's views on the fairer sex. "There's something else I wanted to discuss with you."

His father's eyes narrowed. "What would that be?"

"I want to open a missing-persons division of Vaughn Associates. And I want to do pro bono work, as well as work for hire. As head of the division, I would decide which cases we would take on and which we wouldn't. If you don't want to consider that type of work for this company, then I'll open my own firm to specialize in finding missing persons."

Shock appeared to be the main sentiment on his father's face. "Why would you ever want to do that?"

Concisely Brad explained about Tess Littlehawk and her daughter. Then he added, "I'm flying to California this afternoon to follow up on a lead."

A very long silence echoed in the elegant office. After a long, thoughtful look at Brad, Phillip must have seen his determination and exactly what he'd lose if he dismissed the idea—a connection to his son.

He asked, "Will you put some facts and

figures together and write up a proposal? If you do that, I'll consider it."

A few minutes later, Brad left his father's office and headed toward his own. Maybe he could borrow Emily from Jack just for a day or two. She was so good at collating information.

No, that wouldn't be fair. She was no longer his secretary, and he just had to deal with that. Whenever he thought of Emily, he felt as if he had a hole in his heart. He was trying to fill it by taking his life in a new direction, yet he knew he might have to stop into Jack's office to see her. He might have to tell her his good news.

One of his contacts in California had turned up a shelter log with Annie Littlehawk's name in it. The man had a couple of leads, and Brad wanted to help him chase them down. Soon he'd have to leave for the airport.

When Brad rounded the corner to his office suite, he saw Emily's empty desk. The sight of it made him frown. He didn't even want to think about interviewing for a new personal secretary, but he knew he had to do it.

The white legal-size envelope lying in the

middle of his desk caught his eye as soon as he entered his own office. When he picked it up, he saw his name written on the outside. It was Emily's handwriting.

His heart pounding faster, he took out the typed letter, read it and swore. It was impersonal, one paragraph, a letter of resignation and thanks for all he'd done for her.

There was no explanation for why she'd written it, and he suddenly knew exactly why. She wanted to put him and Thunder Canyon out of her life.

Brad thought about going after her, but what would he say? *I can't stand the thought of coming to work and you not being here? I hate the idea of you working somewhere else?*

With a blinding flash of insight, he realized his feelings had nothing to do with Emily quitting her job. Rather, they had to do with him not seeing her again and not seeing her every day.

What had he thought they were going to do? Have coffee together in the mornings before she went off to work for Jack and he opened his own division?

As Brad packed his bag that afternoon for his trip, he thought about Emily. As he

boarded the plane, he thought about Emily.
As he slept alone in his hotel room that night,
he thought about Emily.

Brad's contact in California had done good
groundwork in San Jose. After two days of
following leads, Brad found Annie Littlehawk in a bookstore shelving books. When
he introduced himself and insisted that her
mother missed her terribly, she began crying.

"I can't go home," she told him as she ordered a soda at a nearby restaurant. She was
a beautiful young woman, with long black
hair and sparkling brown eyes.

"Tell me why not."

After a few moments of hesitation, she
murmured, "It's not just that I ran away. I
know that hurt my mother. But I did things
I'm not proud of *after* I ran."

"Your mother needs to know you're well
and safe. All these years she didn't know if
you were alive or dead. That's heartbreak-
ing for a parent."

"I can't believe she hired you to look for
me. How could she afford that?"

"Let's just say fate put us together at the
right place at the right time. You have to let
her know you're okay."

Annie fingered the straw of her soda. "I didn't think she'd ever want to hear from me again. I caused her so much trouble. We fought all the time. I said things I never should have said."

"You think your mother hasn't made mistakes in her life?"

When Annie looked up at him with wide, miserable eyes, she frowned. "She's a good person. She'd never intentionally hurt someone."

"Did you *want* to hurt her?"

"Yes! Because she wouldn't let me do what I wanted to do. She laid down all these rules and I didn't understand why."

"And now you do?"

Annie nodded.

"Then call her." He slid his business card across the table with Tess's information written on the back. "That's where she's living and working now."

As Annie looked torn, he advised her, "Don't decide right now whether you're going to come home or not. I can tell her I found you, but I'm sure she'd much rather hear from *you*. If you decide you want to fly back to Thunder Canyon, let me know and I'll make the arrangements."

"Why do you care if I go home?" she asked, looking perplexed.

"Because I'm learning how important family is, how important bonds are. You don't break them if you can help it. And if you do and you have a chance to fix them, it's important that you try."

Three hours later, taking the red-eye back to Chicago, Brad thought about his words to Annie. He thought about them as he let himself into his penthouse and felt the emptiness there. Making strong coffee, he didn't even try to get any sleep. There was something he had to do...something he should have done years before.

It was nine-thirty in the morning when he greeted the doorman at his mother's apartment building. After he took the elevator up to her apartment, he rang the bell.

Connie Vaughn was an attractive woman in her early sixties. Her gray hair was silvery and she wore it in a pageboy, as she'd done for years. Today she was dressed in a taupe sweater and slacks and looked more than a little surprised to see him.

"Did I forget a breakfast date?" she asked.

They were long past due for dinner or breakfast or...something. That was *his* fault.

"No, you didn't forget. I need to talk to you. Do you have time?"

Her eyes became worried now. "I always have time for you."

Looking back, he knew that was true.

Going into the elegantly furnished living room, he took a seat on the sofa.

She sat across from him in an upholstered chair and asked, "New look?"

He'd showered and changed but hadn't bothered to shave. "No. I just didn't take the time for the whole works."

"What was so urgent?"

Now that he was here, he didn't quite know how to put it into words. "I've met someone."

His mother smiled. "Is that good or bad?"

"I'm still trying to figure that out. She's different."

"Different in a general sense or different from the women you usually date?"

Connie Vaughn had hit the bull's-eye. "Different from women I usually date. She was my secretary."

He didn't see the disapproval he thought he might as his mother asked, "Was?"

"It's a complicated story. We were in Montana together the last few weeks on a case. She resigned when we came back."

"If she was your secretary, then she doesn't have money."

"No, she doesn't. Money's not important to Emily."

"You're sure of that?"

"I'm positive. She's put her own life on hold so she could help her sisters through school."

"It sounds as if she *needs* money."

"No. I mean, I offered to pay for Emily's own college courses and she wouldn't accept it. She has a lot of pride and self-respect and insists on making her own way. She never coats the truth in pretty words, and I can usually tell what she's feeling," he went on, remembering every detail of their time together.

"Usually?"

"Right now—" Frustrated, he raked his hand through his hair. "I cut things off between us because I didn't think I wanted a wife and a family. Or maybe I just never thought I'd be successful at it and I don't attempt anything I can't succeed at. Now I need some answers. I realize that what happened between you and Dad colored my view of women and marriage and whether or not two people can share a life."

"What answers do you need?" his mother inquired softly.

"Why did you have an affair?"

When Connie stood, she went to the window to look down over the city. "I wish I could give you a *simple* answer, but there isn't one. There is an easy answer, though. Your father didn't give me what I needed."

Now she turned to face Brad. "I know that must sound ridiculous when we had everything money could buy. But I needed the intangible things that maybe women need more than men."

"Such as?"

"Time…attention…affection."

"But you were married!"

She laughed. "Oh, yes. My family had a hand in that. I'd just graduated from college when Phillip's family invited me to come stay with them for a weekend. My father and his father had been old college buddies."

"The marriage was arranged?"

"No, not in any old-world sense. Let's just say we both came highly recommended. At first I was fascinated by your father. He was so intelligent, so sophisticated, five years older than me and worldly. He intrigued me, and I mistook his ambition and drive to succeed for passion."

Not knowing if he wanted to set foot in that arena, Brad decided he needed to have answers. "I don't understand."

"I thought the intensity in Phillip's nature meant he could love deeply, that when he turned his energy on a relationship, it would be everything we both could want."

"But he didn't do that?"

His mother slipped her hands into her slacks pockets. "Your father could build an empire if he wanted to, but he couldn't talk to me. I fell in love with him. I thought if we got married and had a family we'd find what we needed together. That didn't happen. The more he worked, the more distant he became. That distance turned to coldness. He didn't know how to show affection and didn't want to learn. He wouldn't even consider counseling. So our marriage limped along until one day I met someone who looked into my eyes when he talked to me. He put his hand on my shoulder when I needed one there. He listened in a way I'd never been listened to before. I had been drowning emotionally and he saved me. So we had an affair."

"And Dad found out?"

"Yes. One afternoon we weren't careful and had lunch in a popular restaurant. One of your father's associates saw us. I don't know. Maybe I wanted him to find out. Maybe I wanted to push myself into making some kind of decision, and that's what happened."

As Brad honestly thought about his dad, he knew his father could be cold and distant. He'd just never pictured how that would play out in a marriage. He'd blamed his mother all these years for her lack of morals, for her infidelity to her vows. Yet hadn't his father broken their vows before she had by his attitude, by his neglect of her?

"Men-and-women relationships are complicated, Brad. They're never exactly what they seem on the outside," she counseled him.

"After you and Dad divorced, did you see the man you had the affair with?"

"No."

"Why not?"

Now she sat on the sofa again and folded her hands in her lap. "Because of you. I knew what you thought of me. I knew you believed I'd destroyed our family. At first you were resentful and defiant and sullen. I couldn't get a smile out of you for months. Do you honestly think I would have taken a chance on losing you altogether by dating and maybe marrying this man?"

Never before had Brad realized what his mother had sacrificed for him. He thought about Emily and what she'd sacrificed for her sisters. Was that kind of selflessness in women's natures?

Not all women. Just the special ones.

"What about now? Why haven't you ever gotten married?"

"Cowardice, I guess. And I've become set in my ways." She studied him for a few moments. "But I know *you* have more courage than I do. I also know you've dated a lot of wrong women, and maybe that's why you've never asked me these questions before."

"Emily makes me think and question. She makes me laugh. She frustrates me, yet she leads me to see life in a different way. And…I love her. I *do* love her." He could admit that now.

"Did you say she resigned?"

"Yes, and she's hurt because I cut her out of my life. She has no reason to ever want to speak to me again."

"But you're going to find a reason."

Ever since he'd read Emily's resignation

letter, he'd felt as if he had a lead weight in his chest. Now he felt lighter.

"Yes. I'm going to find that reason."

On Sunday afternoon, Emily was looking at the pictures she'd shot in Montana and the want ads lying beside her on the sofa. She had three interviews set up for Friday. She had intended to look through the paper, circling more possibilities. But she'd picked up her developed pictures yesterday and she couldn't seem to put them away. The breathtaking Montana scenery tugged at a deep place in her soul. However, the pictures of Brad brought tears to her eyes. Her heart hurt and she didn't know if she'd ever get over him.

Reluctantly plopping the pictures on the coffee table, she picked up the newspaper, intent on finding a new job, when her phone rang.

"Hello? This is Emily Stanton."

"Emily? It's Brad."

Her heart pounded so fast, she couldn't catch her breath. Was he calling so she'd reconsider her resignation?

"Emily?"

"I'm here," she managed to say.

"I want you to fly to Thunder Canyon with me tomorrow."

"Tomorrow?"

"Yes."

"Why?"

"To finish what we started. A couple of things have happened. I found Tess's daughter. Annie's going to fly in and she and Tess are going to be reunited. I want to keep *that* meeting private. But then there's going to be a press conference, and the mayor would like both of us there."

"Why a press conference?"

"The deed was authenticated. Lisa Martin is the true owner of the Queen of Hearts mine. Apparently this story has piqued the nation's interest, and the press conference will be broadcast on CNN. The other networks might be there, too. Brookhurst says he'll tell us what he has planned when we get there, but he's adamant about you coming along. You're the one who found the deed."

"It was a fluke."

"A fluke *you* investigated. The mayor wants us *both* there," he repeated firmly.

When Brad used that tone, she knew he wouldn't change his mind. "And you want to leave tomorrow?"

"Yes. We'll have a meeting with the mayor after we arrive. The press conference will be held the following morning. Will you come along and finish this with me?"

She knew she shouldn't. She knew her heart was already broken and being with Brad would keep it that way. Yet she also couldn't resist the idea of seeing him again, being with him again. Besides, she did want to see Tess and her daughter reunited. That was the most important aspect of all this.

"All right. I'll come along."

There was a pause. Then he said, "Great. I have meetings tomorrow morning before our flight so I'll send a car for you."

"I can take a taxi."

"I'll send a car for you. He'll pick you up around nine-thirty. Our flight leaves at noon."

Before she had a chance to change her mind, he hung up.

Gazing at the pictures she'd taken of Brad, she knew this could be the biggest mistake of her life. Nevertheless, she had nothing to lose this time because she'd already lost her heart.

On *this* trip when Emily and Brad arrived in Bozeman, he rented a car. The awkwardness between them had hit an all-time high. Brad seemed to be mulling something over, and she'd left him to his thoughts most of the trip.

Now, as they drove into Thunder Canyon for their meeting with the mayor, she asked, "Are we going to check in at the motel first?"

"We're not staying at the motel."

"We certainly won't be welcome at the Lazy D."

"Actually, we're staying at the cabin tonight."

Her gaze jerked toward his. "Why?"

"The same reason as last time, actually. Everything's booked up. This press conference has brought people in from all over the country, including reporters, news teams and curious busybodies."

"And Caleb's letting us use the cabin?"

"I made a deal with him."

That surprised Emily. Last week she might have asked Brad what the deal was. But today she really had no right to know.

The meeting with the mayor was methodical as he went over the schedule for the press conference.

Then Brad said, "I'm picking up someone at the airport tomorrow morning. Is there a place we could use to have a private meeting before the press conference starts?"

The mayor thought about it. "You can use Conference Room A on the second floor. Would that be suitable?"

"That will be just fine."

Emily couldn't help but see that Brad looked worried. Maybe he was afraid Tess and her daughter's reunion wouldn't go well.

As they drove to the cabin, Emily asked, "I guess the creek water's gone down?"

"Yep. I had someone check it for us. Unless we get tons of rain overnight, we'll be able to get out in the morning." His gaze met hers. "Don't you want to get stranded again?"

She wasn't exactly sure how to answer that one. "I have job interviews on Friday. I can't miss those."

When Brad looked back at the road, his jaw was set, his mouth a tight line. Something was going on with him, but she had no idea what it was.

After they arrived at the cabin, she saw it was stocked both with groceries and with firewood. Apparently Brad wasn't taking any chances this time.

She motioned toward the logs. "We have plenty."

Dropping his suitcase next to the sofa, Brad motioned out back. "There's a generator hooked up now, too, so you won't have to worry about the power going out."

"I'm not worried." She wasn't—not as long as she was with Brad.

After they'd eaten a quiet supper with forced conversation, Brad realized he didn't know what the hell he was doing. He thought he'd planned this out, but being with Emily again had made him doubt his course. He didn't want her to think he'd brought her to the cabin again to sleep with her. That wasn't what this was about. But she seemed as jittery as a teenager on her first date, and he wasn't much better. He knew he couldn't just tell Emily he loved her. He had to show her. He had to make a public declaration so she'd know his intentions were true.

Tomorrow he'd find out if she loved him. If she wanted to spend her life with him. The suspense was killing him.

They sat in front of the fire listening to music. He told her how he'd found Tess's daughter and then he added, "I'm going to take more cases like Tess's."

"Missing persons?"

"Yes. Especially parents who can't find

their kids. I'm starting a new division at Vaughn Associates just for that."

Her eyes became huge and wide. "Your father agreed to that?"

"He didn't have much choice if he wanted me to stay. I'll be head of the division. He won't be overseeing it."

Emily looked happy for him, yet there was deep sadness in her eyes, too, and he wondered if that was because they wouldn't be working together. They might be if all went as he'd planned.

As Emily stared into the fire for a few more moments, she said, "I guess I'd better turn in."

He hadn't touched her up until now because his self-control was at a premium. Although he wanted her in his arms, he wanted her there the *right* way.

When she stood, he stood with her and blocked her path to the bedroom. "Did you see the gossip column in the newspaper a few days ago—about Suzette and me?"

"Yes, I did. It was a public statement that you're not the father of Suzette Brouchard's child. I guess you're glad that's all over."

"I am. I just wanted you to know it was cleared up."

"Brad, I'm sorry I didn't believe you at first. My only excuse is that I didn't know you. Once we spent time in Thunder Canyon together, I realized that if you said you weren't the father, then you weren't the father. I knew that before we returned to Chicago."

Grateful Emily would never be anything but honest with him, he was touched deeply by her words. His lips longed to take a kiss, his hands longed to rove her body, but instead of doing either, he brought his hands to her shoulders and leaned in and kissed her forehead.

Huskily he said, "You have sweet dreams tonight, Emily. You should never have any other kind."

As she looked up at him questioningly, he just smiled and tapped his index finger to her nose.

Smiling back, she disappeared into the bedroom and closed the door.

Chapter Fourteen

When Emily took Tess to breakfast the following morning, Caleb's housekeeper was outwardly nervous. She couldn't seem to sit still, opening her purse for a tissue, pushing her food around, picking up her fork and putting it down again, wiping her mouth with her napkin.

Emily leaned across the table and patted her arm. "It's going to be all right."

"When I talked to Annie on Saturday, she seemed so hesitant about coming home again. I told her it didn't have to be permanently. If she liked California, I could go out there and visit her. Since Mr. Vaughn won't take any money for finding Annie, I have my savings."

"Your daughter might need to get the feel of Thunder Canyon again. I know it took *me* a while."

"She wasn't happy here," Tess said with a shake of her head. "Maybe I should move out there. I could. Maybe Mr. Douglas has a friend in California I could work for." Then she sighed. "He's still in such a bad mood these days because of the mine and all."

Ignoring Tess's comment about Caleb, Emily focused on Annie. "I think you should wait and spend a few days with your daughter and find out what she's thinking. You'll have to get to know each other all over again."

Tess took another bite of her eggs. "I guess you're right. My mind's just speeding ahead so fast I can't stop it."

All too well Emily knew what that was like. Last night as she'd lain in the cabin bedroom alone, hearing Brad move about out in the living room, her mind had raced, too. But it hadn't gotten anywhere.

She wondered why he'd asked her along. Simply because she'd been involved in the case and might want to see the conclusion?

Although he'd told her the mayor wanted her there, that seemed superficial. Maybe this trip was Brad's way of saying a final good-bye since they hadn't done it when she'd resigned. Whatever the reason, her heart ached to be with him…really with him. He'd driven into Bozeman to pick up Annie at the airport, and she and Tess were supposed to meet him at the town hall in the conference room upstairs at ten-thirty. The press conference was scheduled for eleven.

Glancing around the Hitching Post, trying to absorb everything about it because she knew she wouldn't be back, Emily felt tears come to her eyes. Not wanting Tess to see, she quickly blinked them away, winked at the Shady Lady above the bar—a woman who'd had a lot more substance than the town had ever expected—and said to Tess, "I don't want to rush you, but we should be going."

Pushing back her plate, Tess gave Emily a weak smile. "Thank you for the breakfast. I just wasn't hungry."

Emily had taken care of the bill after the waitress had brought their breakfast. Now she left a tip and led Tess outside.

It was a beautiful end of May day, and the

immense blue sky was cloudless. The temperature was already sixty degrees, and Emily's light blazer felt just right. She'd bought the pantsuit for her job interviews. It was a beautiful emerald-green, and the sea-foam blouse complemented it. Brad had appraised her that morning with a light in his eyes that usually meant he wanted to kiss her. But he hadn't.

She wouldn't think about that.

That morning Brad had dropped off Emily and Tess at the Hitching Post. Now they strolled leisurely through Old Town to the town hall. Already residents, tourists and news crews were spilling from the covered sidewalk into the street. The mayor had given both Emily and Brad passes so security would allow them inside.

Emily showed her pass to the security guard, keeping hold of Tess's arm. "She's with me," Emily said.

After the guard gave Tess the once-over, he nodded for them to enter.

Sitting at her desk, Rhonda fielded questions from men in suits and ties and women professionally attired. She'd be busy today.

Emily guided Tess toward the staircase to the left of the large foyer. It was the same polished wood as the floor, and Emily caught the scent of must and history as they neared the second-floor landing. Going down a hall, she spotted Conference Room A and opened the door. No one was inside.

With all her heart Emily hoped that Annie hadn't changed her mind and decided not to fly to Thunder Canyon.

There was a conference table and a few chairs, but Tess went to stand at the window. "All this fuss over a gold mine. Don't these people know what's really important?"

Emily knew what Tess meant. She knew what was important. Loving someone was important. "Lisa Martin's life might change completely because of this."

"Maybe not for the better," Tess murmured.

When the door to the conference room suddenly opened, Emily saw Brad first. He quickly stepped aside, letting a pretty young girl pass him.

Annie Littlehawk stood immobile in the doorway for a few seconds. Then Tess opened her arms to her daughter and Annie flew into them. Both women were crying, and Emily felt tears on her cheeks, too.

Crossing to the door, she gave Brad a wide

smile. He put his arm around her shoulders, drawing her close.

Then he said in a husky voice, "Tess, Annie, you can stay here as long as you want. We're going to leave and give you some privacy. Mr. Douglas said he would send a car when you're ready to go back to the Lazy D. Just call the ranch."

When he and Emily were standing in the hall with the door closed, Emily smiled up at him. "I'm so proud of you for finding Annie."

"I had help." Taking his arm from around Emily's shoulders, he nodded downstairs. "We'd better get to the press conference. Mayor Brookhurst won't be happy if we're late."

When Emily and Brad entered the huge reception room, the mayor was already on the stage at the west end of the hall. He beckoned to them. After they mounted the steps, he murmured, "I can't get in touch with Lisa Martin, and no one knows where she is. I guess she'll find out she's the owner if she has her television tuned in to CNN."

There was a podium on the stage, which the mayor went to after he motioned Emily and Brad to the two chairs also on the stage.

There was a handheld mike on a stand beside one of the chairs that they could pass from one to the other.

As soon as the mayor tapped on the podium, the room went silent and all eyes were upon him. He introduced himself, knowing full well network cameras were shooting close-ups. Then he welcomed everyone and gave them a brief history of Thunder Canyon. However, he kept his speech short.

Finally he motioned to Brad. "Mr. Vaughn, a private investigator from Chicago, will now tell you how he and his assistant found the actual deed to the Queen of Hearts gold mine."

Emily noticed that Brad seemed very comfortable with the microphone as he made eye contact with the reporters and residents of Thunder Canyon, relating how he and Emily had investigated the ownership of the mine up until their visit with Tildy Matheson. Then he handed the mike to Emily, and she spoke about the trunk in Tildy's attic and the torn lining. The crowd listened with hushed fascination. Finally, when Emily had finished, Brad nodded to the mayor, and Brookhurst handed him something from inside the podium. It looked like a framed picture.

But it wasn't a photograph. Emily soon saw it was the deed, preserved and framed so nothing would happen to it.

The mayor announced, "The legal owner of the Queen of Hearts gold mine will be presented with this deed at the first opportunity."

"Who *is* the owner?" a reporter shouted out.

"The rightful owner of the mine was Lily Divine. According to our research, her great-great-granddaughter, Lisa Martin, will now inherit it."

Questions exploded. Many of them, about Lisa, couldn't be answered. Emily suspected reporters would be knocking on Tildy's door, as well as Lisa Martin's, as soon as the press conference was over.

As the questions eventually subsided, the mayor turned to Brad. "As far as the Queen of Hearts gold mine is concerned, we've concluded that part of the press conference. But Mr. Vaughn has something else he'd like to say."

Suddenly Brad stood with the microphone. Instead of addressing the audience, however, he turned toward Emily. Taking her hand, he drew her up out of her chair.

"Brad, what are you doing?" she whispered frantically.

"What I'm doing is acknowledging how I feel about you in front of the whole world."

Her heart galloped at triple speed as she looked up into his eyes, stunned by his announcement.

"I want the whole world to know how very special you are and how very much I love you. It was our trip to Thunder Canyon that made me realize how wonderful you are and how much I need you in my life."

Then he took a box from his pocket and knelt before her on one knee!

The room was silent again, everyone looking on and listening as Brad went on. "I'm taking the biggest risk of my life here today, Emily, because I don't know what you're going to say. But I felt I had to propose this way to prove to you how much I care about you. Pretty words don't mean a thing without action. So I'm taking action."

Opening the box, he held out a beautiful diamond in an antique white-gold setting. "I love you, Emily Stanton, and I want you to be my wife. Will you marry me?"

No words came to mind as tears welled up in her eyes. She looked at the ring and then she gazed at Brad kneeling on the floor before her…humbling himself before her. All at once she realized he'd planned his proposal this way to prove to her he didn't care if she was from a different background. He didn't care that her father had been a blue-collar worker. He didn't care that she didn't move in his social circle. He was on his knee before her to prove how very much he loved her.

Somehow she found the words she needed to banish the anxiety in his eyes, to assure him she felt the same way he did. "Yes, I'll marry you."

At her answer he was on his feet and folding her into his arms, kissing her with all the pent-up passion he'd been holding in check.

Applause rang out all around them.

When Brad broke away from her, he took the ring from the box and slipped it onto her finger. Then he took her hand, led her from the stage and on a dash through the reporters and residents of Thunder Canyon. They were going too fast for anyone to stop them.

She ran beside him to the parking lot, asking, "Where are we going?"

"To the cabin."

"I can't believe Caleb is letting you use it again."

Two reporters followed them and were now close on their heels. Brad said, "I'll explain after we get there. Come on."

In seconds they'd hopped into the SUV and pulled out of the parking lot with a screech of tires.

They veered onto Thunder Canyon Road. Still stunned, Emily mused, "I thought we were going back to Chicago today."

"Can you spare a few days with me? We have a lot to talk about."

Happiness began in her heart and filled her whole being. "I can spare a *lifetime* for you."

Taking her hand again, he laid it on his thigh, and that's where it stayed while they drove to the cabin.

Once there, they climbed out of the car and went to the doorstep.

Brad scooped her into his arms. "Finally," he sighed.

"Finally what?" she asked with a coy grin.

"Finally you're mine."

She held her ring up to the sunlight. "Is that what this means?"

"You can bet your life that's what it means."

Opening the cabin door, he carried her over the threshold. After he kicked it shut with his foot, he took her to the bedroom and gently set her on the bed. With a quick shrug he ridded himself of his suit coat, then unknotted his tie and tossed them both to the bedside chair.

Beside her on the bed, he held her face in his hands. "Do you know how much I love you?"

"Tell me," she murmured.

"It about drove me nuts last night to sleep here with you and not sleep *with* you. I wanted you to know this trip had nothing to do with sex. This trip was about you and me and the life we're going to have…the children we're going to have. We're going to spend a few days here planning and dreaming because this is *our* cabin now."

"You're kidding!"

"Nope. I made an offer Caleb couldn't refuse. This is going to be our getaway when life gets too demanding. It will be our vacation spot. When we have kids, I guess we'll have to build on to it."

After he helped rid Emily of her jacket, he began unbuttoning her blouse.

Her fingers worked at the buttons of his shirt. "What made you change your mind? About marriage, I mean. That night at my mom's apartment you seemed so definite—"

His fingers stilled. "I was definite because I was denying what I felt. I thought if I sounded definite I'd be able to convince myself. When I walked away from you that night, my heart hurt, and when I found your resignation on my desk, I knew I couldn't abide the thought of you being with anybody but me. I went to find Tess's daughter and realized how important family was. After I came back, I had a long talk with my mother and I understood things I'd never understood before."

"About your parents' breakup?"

Tenderly he took her hand in his and caressed her palm. "Yes. She sacrificed her happiness to keep me in her life. I think over the last couple of years I realized that cars and trips and work couldn't bring happiness. I was restless and dissatisfied and unfulfilled until I came here and got to know you. Then my attitude and perspective changed. Maybe I finally grew up."

Seriously he said, "I know I put you on the spot at the press conference. If you have any doubts about marrying me, any doubts at all, we'll wait until I've proven to you there are no reasons for doubts."

During their stay in Thunder Canyon,

Emily had learned that Brad was a man of integrity, a kind man, one who would know the value of a vow and stand by one for the rest of his life. "I don't have any doubts."

"If you want to go to college, we can make sure that happens. If you want to work with me and find missing persons, I'd like that a lot."

"I've been thinking about getting my private investigator's license. Working with you sounds like a wonderful idea. I'm absolutely sure about our future together. I do have one request, though."

"What?"

"Will you make love to me until I believe everything that happened today is real?"

"Your wish is my command."

Then Brad was kissing her and holding her and undressing her and loving her.

Emily's dream burned away in the fire of their passion, and she wasn't sorry. Because the reality of Brad loving her was so much better than any dream ever could be.

* * * * *

YES! Please send me **The Montana Mavericks Collection** in Larger Print. This collection begins with 3 FREE books and 2 FREE gifts (gifts valued at approx. $20.00 retail) in the first shipment, along with the other first 4 books from the collection! If I do not cancel, I will receive 8 monthly shipments until I have the entire 51-book Montana Mavericks collection. I will receive 2 or 3 FREE books in each shipment and I will pay just $4.99 US/ $5.89 CDN for each of the other four books in each shipment, plus $2.99 for shipping and handling per shipment.*If I decide to keep the entire collection, I'll have paid for only 32 books, because 19 books are FREE! I understand that accepting the 3 free books and gifts places me under no obligation to buy anything. I can always return a shipment and cancel at any time. My free books and gifts are mine to keep no matter what I decide.

263 HCN 2404   463 HCN 2404

Name	(PLEASE PRINT)	
Address		Apt. #
City	State/Prov.	Zip/Postal Code

Signature (if under 18, a parent or guardian must sign)

Mail to the **Reader Service:**

IN U.S.A.: P.O. Box 1867, Buffalo, NY 14240-1867
IN CANADA: P.O. Box 609, Fort Erie, Ontario L2A 5X3

* Terms and prices subject to change without notice. Prices do not include applicable taxes. Sales tax applicable in N.Y. Canadian residents will be charged applicable taxes. This offer is limited to one order per household. All orders subject to approval. Credit or debit balances in a customer's account(s) may be offset by any other outstanding balance owed by or to the customer. Please allow 4 to 6 weeks for delivery. Offer available while quantities last. Offer not available to Quebec residents.

REQUEST YOUR FREE BOOKS!

2 FREE NOVELS PLUS 2 FREE GIFTS!

HARLEQUIN

SPECIAL EDITION

Life, Love & Family

YES! Please send me 2 FREE Harlequin® Special Edition novels and my 2 FREE gifts (gifts are worth about $10). After receiving them, if I don't wish to receive any more books, I can return the shipping statement marked "cancel." If I don't cancel, I will receive 6 brand-new novels every month and be billed just $4.74 per book in the U.S. or $5.24 per book in Canada. That's a savings of at least 14% off the cover price! It's quite a bargain! Shipping and handling is just 50¢ per book in the U.S. and 75¢ per book in Canada.* I understand that accepting the 2 free books and gifts places me under no obligation to buy anything. I can always return a shipment and cancel at any time. Even if I never buy another book, the two free books and gifts are mine to keep forever.

235/335 HDN F46C

Name	(PLEASE PRINT)

Address		Apt. #

City	State/Prov.	Zip/Postal Code

Signature (if under 18, a parent or guardian must sign)

Mail to the **Harlequin® Reader Service:**
IN U.S.A.: P.O. Box 1867, Buffalo, NY 14240-1867
IN CANADA: P.O. Box 609, Fort Erie, Ontario L2A 5X3

Want to try two free books from another line?
Call 1-800-873-8635 or visit www.ReaderService.com.

* Terms and prices subject to change without notice. Prices do not include applicable taxes. Sales tax applicable in N.Y. Canadian residents will be charged applicable taxes. Offer not valid in Quebec. This offer is limited to one order per household. Not valid for current subscribers to Harlequin Special Edition books. All orders subject to credit approval. Credit or debit balances in a customer's account(s) may be offset by any other outstanding balance owed by or to the customer. Please allow 4 to 6 weeks for delivery. Offer available while quantities last.

Your Privacy—The Harlequin® Reader Service is committed to protecting your privacy. Our Privacy Policy is available online at www.ReaderService.com or upon request from the Harlequin Reader Service.

We make a portion of our mailing list available to reputable third parties that offer products we believe may interest you. If you prefer that we not exchange your name with third parties, or if you wish to clarify or modify your communication preferences, please visit us at www.ReaderService.com/consumerchoice or write to us at Harlequin Reader Service Preference Service, P.O. Box 9062, Buffalo, NY 14269. Include your complete name and address.

HSEDIR13R

REQUEST YOUR FREE BOOKS!
2 FREE NOVELS PLUS 2 FREE GIFTS!

♦ HARLEQUIN

American ★ Romance®

LOVE, HOME & HAPPINESS

YES! Please send me 2 FREE Harlequin® American Romance® novels and my 2 FREE gifts (gifts are worth about $10). After receiving them, if I don't wish to receive any more books, I can return the shipping statement marked "cancel." If I don't cancel, I will receive 4 brand-new novels every month and be billed just $4.74 per book in the U.S. or $5.24 per book in Canada. That's a savings of at least 14% off the cover price! It's quite a bargain! Shipping and handling is just 50¢ per book in the U.S. and 75¢ per book in Canada.* I understand that accepting the 2 free books and gifts places me under no obligation to buy anything. I can always return a shipment and cancel at any time. Even if I never buy another book, the two free books and gifts are mine to keep forever.

154/354 HDN F4YY

Name	(PLEASE PRINT)

Address	Apt. #

City	State/Prov.	Zip/Postal Code

Signature (if under 18, a parent or guardian must sign)

Mail to the **Harlequin**® Reader Service:
IN U.S.A.: P.O. Box 1867, Buffalo, NY 14240-1867
IN CANADA: P.O. Box 609, Fort Erie, Ontario L2A 5X3

Want to try two free books from another line?
Call 1-800-873-8635 or visit www.ReaderService.com.

* Terms and prices subject to change without notice. Prices do not include applicable taxes. Sales tax applicable in N.Y. Canadian residents will be charged applicable taxes. Offer not valid in Quebec. This offer is limited to one order per household. Not valid for current subscribers to Harlequin American Romance books. All orders subject to credit approval. Credit or debit balances in a customer's account(s) may be offset by any other outstanding balance owed by or to the customer. Please allow 4 to 6 weeks for delivery. Offer available while quantities last.

Your Privacy—The Harlequin® Reader Service is committed to protecting your privacy. Our Privacy Policy is available online at www.ReaderService.com or upon request from the Harlequin Reader Service.

We make a portion of our mailing list available to reputable third parties that offer products we believe may interest you. If you prefer that we not exchange your name with third parties, or if you wish to clarify or modify your communication preferences, please visit us at www.ReaderService.com/consumerschoice or write to us at Harlequin Reader Service Preference Service, P.O. Box 9062, Buffalo, NY 14269. Include your complete name and address.

HARDIR13R